ACKNOWLEDGMENTS

My son, Mark, insisted that I publish this book. So there.

I could not have written it without the help of Anne, my beautiful and talented wife. She encouraged me and put up with me. Anne read the book and gave me not only her comments, but thoughtful changes. Her questions and suggestions stretched me and made this book more than it was. It was a long, hard pull.

My dear friend, Elaine Kendall was a great reader and an inspiration. She is an extraordinary woman and one of the true literati. Judge George Eskin gave me assistance with my wandering legal terms, spelling and grammar. It is always a shock to remember what I've forgotten. My buddy, Chuck Kay. was generous with his time and comments.

And finally, Noah Ben Shea, a great writer, philosopher and poet, provided me with his humor and his insight. Some of the words and phrases here are his. The better ones, no doubt.

Desperate Shop Girls

BY

David L. Gersh

A James Emerson Harris Matter

Printed in the United States of America.

For information address:

PRIDES CROSSING PRESS
PO Box 50647
Santa Barbara, CA 93150

Library of Congress Cataloging-in-Publication Data

Gersh, David L.

DESPERATE SHOP GIRLS/David L. Gersh

ISBN: 0692389210
ISBN-13: 978-0692389218

For Anne

Also by David Gersh

Art is Dead

Going, Going, Gone

Chapter 1

I read the State Bar Discipline Reports like some people read the obituaries. I have to make sure my legal career didn't die while I was sleeping. It's not as easy as you might think. Not when you've got my luck. Like the current mess I'm in.

My name is James Emerson Harris. Everyone calls me Jimmy. I'm 44 and I still have the body God gave me. Well, actually that body departed about four years ago and I have the body I suppose I deserve. I like to think my boyish, lopsided grin and my blond hair make up for it. Oh, and my baby blue eyes.

I've been in San Buenasera for seven years now. I moved up from L.A. after I had the go-around with the State Bar. Mid-life crisis. It really wasn't that serious. Besides, I've been on the wagon for the last six years. Almost. Anyway, this whole thing started about six months ago.

It was Christmas time. That means it was 68 degrees and sunny. Hey, it doesn't snow in Bethlehem either.

Janet Mason is a brunette. A real knockout. I'd like to say this right up front. I didn't mean to kill her. It was an accident.

I was at my desk, as I usually am at 10 o'clock in the morning. I'm not much of a morning person, but I have my standards. We have a view of the harbor from the little house I rent as an office. I'd been looking out the window.

I do that a lot. There's this little sloop. I figure maybe 36 feet. Bruno was on my lap, looking too. He's a long-haired dachshund. I don't let him use the binoculars.

There's always some girl around the boat. Sunbathing or cleaning up. Usually topless. This one had really nice firm tits. Little pink nipples pointing up. She was wearing a Santa hat. It was cheery.

The girls change every week or two. The strange thing is, I've never seen a guy on the boat. Go figure. I made another mental note to investigate. My follow-through sucks sometimes.

Anyway, my secretary, assistant, receptionist, Pamela buzzed me on the intercom. "Mr. Harris, there's a client here to see you. A Ms. Mason. May I send her in?" That was unusual. She usually calls me Jimmy. This woman must have impressed her.

I slipped my binoculars back in the bottom drawer and moved my knees apart a little. Bruno gave me a hurt look, then crawled down off my lap and waddled over to the couch. He jumped up, which for Bruno is a full day's exercise. He made a little circle and settled in, facing me. Bruno likes to watch.

I stood up and a woman, maybe 5'7", around 33 years old came in. Gray eyes. As I said, a great looker. Expensive, well tailored clothes. Terrific dark hair, beautifully cut. But there was something about her I couldn't quite put my finger on.

I extended my hand. "I'm James Harris."

"Janet Mason," she said, taking my hand.

"Please have a seat." I held the client chair out for her. She sat down and crossed her legs. Lots of legs. Then she smoothed her short skirt and looked up at me and smiled. She had a killer smile. Perfect white teeth. They all showed.

She looked over towards Bruno. "Nice dog," she said.

I staggered around my desk and got successfully back into my chair without making a fool of myself. "How can I help you, Ms. Mason?"

She fingered the string of pearls around the neck of her yellow silk blouse. The diamond she was wearing on her finger flashed in the sunlight. It must have been six carats. I was surprised she could lift it.

"You can tear out my husband's heart for starters." Then she gave me that smile again.

"Ah. I take it you don't like your husband."

"They said you were smart."

"And exactly how would you like me to go about this task?"

"Look, Mr. Harris, let's be serious." She unfolded herself and leaned forward. I got a flash of terrific cleavage. "I want a divorce. I want to get what's coming to me. And I want to hurt the son of a bitch. Not just with the divorce. I want to screw him up badly." An ugly look licked at her face. It shook me.

I've been around for a few years. It wasn't as strange a request as it sounds. Anyway, judging by her clothes and jewelry, it could be a lucrative legal matter.

Usually clients get uptight about my legal bills after the first one. No matter how deeply they feel their moral indignation. Two bills at the most. Except in a divorce where the money comes out of the husband. The only problem was getting hubby to actually pay up. But I could handle that.

"Tell me about yourself, Ms. Mason."

"Don't you recognize me?" Her voice hardened.

That was the moment when Pamela knocked on the door, thank God. She came in and placed a note on my desk. This was unusual.

Pamela is a large woman. She rarely gets up from her desk, except in extremis. All the time she was in my office she couldn't take her eyes off Janet Mason. There was a hint there somewhere. But I hadn't a clue. I gave Janet Mason my best boyish grin and shook my head.

"I use the name Janet Sullivan on television," she said. Her tone wasn't chummy. "'Desperate Shop Girls'? We were on for five years."

"Of course," I said. "I knew you looked familiar. I just couldn't place you. Great show." I made a mental note to look up "Desperate Shop Girls". I'd never heard of it. I'm not much for watching television. I'd rather sit in a room with Karen and read.

I must not have been enthusiastic enough. The corners of Ms. Mason mouth turned down. She didn't look so pretty. "Let's get on with this, Mr. Harris."

"Sure. How'd you get my name?"

"Tony Thompson told me about you." Anthony Thompson, C.P.A. was an accountant here in town. His office was right down the street. There are only four C.P.A.s in San Buenasera, so I take two to lunch a week. There are more accountants in San Luis Obispo up the coast. And Santa Barbara is full of them, but they don't refer matters to a lawyer in San Buenasera. Snobs. To tell you the truth, I wouldn't either. But I've got to make a living so I hustle. Sometimes it pays off.

"I hope he told you how good I am."

"Look, Mr. Harris. I suppose you're competent. At least I hope so. But the important thing is that you're so insignificant that Guy couldn't have bought you. They call it a conflict of interest, don't they? When you represent Guy or one of his companies."

It was comforting to know my reputation preceded me. "I don't get it," I said.

"Don't you know who Guy Mason is? The Guy Mason."

"No."

"Have you been living in a hole somewhere? Don't you have television or newspapers in this little jerk-water town?" I knew I should have been more enthusiastic about "Desperate Shop Girls".

I was beginning to see a side of Ms. Mason that I didn't particularly like. But I looked at her jewelry again, calculated my bank balance and figured out when the rent was due. I decided to ignore my displeasure.

"Why don't you tell me about Mr. Mason so we can both hate him."

She was still incredulous. "You've never heard of Mason Development? Or Guy Mason Construction? Or Mason-Green Real Estate?

"Can't say that I have."

"Amazing." She shook her head. It made her dark hair sway around her face. Her red lips were threaded into a tight line. No more Ms. nice girl. "Guy has developed, built and sold half the houses and apartment buildings between here and Orange County."

"I lead a sheltered life." No pun intended.

To be honest, I don't own any real estate. I used to own a house but that now belongs to Karen. She's my office manager. And my ex-wife. It was an accident. I'm trying to remedy that.

"Are you interested or not, Mr. Harris?" She spoke sharply. A little peckish, I thought. Probably hadn't torn out anyone's heart all morning. I was glad there was a desk between us. But she was reaching for her checkbook.

I cocked an eyebrow. I'm good at that. I practice it in front of a mirror. "Of course. It sounds like an interesting matter. Maybe we should get started."

I have a bad habit. I'm interested in how people use everyday phrases and idioms. Where idioms come from. When I hear one I don't know about, I write it down and research it. Maybe some day I'll write a book. I think it's because I completely missed my salad days. Today's idiom was "Money isn't everything."

Chapter 2

I slowly stroked Karen's leg. We were lying in bed naked. The window was open a crack and we could hear the low rumble of the trucks tearing by on the 101 two blocks up. Puffs of moist wind stirred the curtains. It was going to rain soon.

Karen has a good body to lie naked with. Small and lithe. She rolled over towards me and took my face in her hands and kissed me. I recognized this as a good sign and so did my manly parts. Particularly when she kissed my chest and continued kissing her way down.

I don't think I whimpered. Sighed maybe. Whimpering is for, well -— wimps. I haven't been a wimp since college. Anyway, it felt good. I put my hands on Karen's hair and caught a smell of soapy cleanness. Then I drifted off into happy land.

Karen's 34 now. I've mentioned she's my ex-wife. I've also mentioned it was an accident. It's enough to make you hate lawyers, present company excepted.

Karen and I have a great relationship. We live together. She just doesn't want to get married again.

She didn't want to get divorced either. It was about three years ago. We'd been married for eight years. I fell off the wagon. Hey, I was under a lot of pressure. But Karen is a zero-tolerance kind of lady. No enabling. Those were the rules. So she gave me a chance to get clean and then she got a lawyer up in San Luis Obispo and filed for legal separation. This jerk couldn't even check the right box.

It's a printed form for God's sake. He checked the box for divorce, not legal separation. I moved out and when I got hold of myself, I moved back in. Karen asked for a set of the legal papers a year later. She's like that. Thorough. Right on top of the stack of papers in the file was the final divorce decree. We had a good laugh over a glass of white wine. Hers, not mine. I drink non-alcoholic beer. Then she got this look in her eyes.

My mother hasn't been any help. She takes Karen's side. They have a conspiracy against me. You'd think my mother would want grand-kids.

Since the divorce, I've proposed to Karen at least 15 times. She smiles and kisses me. Sometimes she'll drag me off to the bedroom. But she never says yes. She smiles that great smile and says "Maybe." She's driving me nuts.

But back to tonight. Warm, wet feelings were running up and down me like a choo-choo in a roundhouse. Karen kept making these little mewing sounds as the covers bounced up and down. Then I started thrashing around and making a lot of noise too. She stayed put for a minute or so, then peeked out from under the covers and gave me that incredible smile.

The sheet framed her pretty, pixyish face. Gamine cut red-hair. A light dusting of freckles across her nose, a little darker under her eyes. Big green eyes. Not hazel.

Green with gold specks. The freckles make them look bigger. I drew her to my chest.

I must have drifted off because I awoke with a start when Karen spoke to me. "Who's the new client? Pamela said she's a movie star."

"Television. Did you ever hear of a show called 'Desperate Shop Girls'?"

"Sure. It was a big show a few years back. Why?" She snuggled up against me and put her head on my chest.

"That's the show she starred in. Success doesn't seem to have given her a good disposition."

"Touchy?"

I looked down at the pretty crown of red head. I'd say more bitchy."

She looked up at me. "Don't speak of the clients that way, dear. It isn't good manners." She said it with a smile, which is good.

I stuck out my tongue. I do that to bait her. She socked me in the arm. Ouch. She's stronger than she looks.

Bruno scratched at the door. I think Karen likes me better than Bruno, but I'm not sure. She got up and padded naked across the floor. She's got a great tush.

Bruno dashed in at light speed for a long-haired dachshund and tried to hop up on the bed. He made it half way up the side. Karen leaned down and lifted him up. He licked her hand. He didn't lick me. I hate suck-ups.

"So, what's with this woman?" she said bounding back onto the bed. You can't distract Karen. A gust of wet wind blew the curtains back. "Brrr." she said and dug back under the covers.

"She wants a divorce. And she wants me to sue to stop the new development up on the hill." I didn't bother to tell her the reasons Janet Mason gave me.

"What development?"

"Our Mr. Mason, Janet's soon to be erstwhile husband, bought the old Franklin Farms. All 1400 acres of it. He's going to develop it into a gated community."

"I haven't heard about that." I hadn't heard about it either until Janet Mason told me. And this is a very small town. Somebody worked hard at being quiet about it.

"It's a big secret. They want to have plans done before word gets out. I guess they want to soften up the City Council." I think our City Council was imported directly from Chicago. Softening is possible.

"What do you know about land use law?"

"Hey. I'm a great attorney. I can do anything." Yeah. Sure. Besides, I was having Clyde do the research. Clyde's our paralegal. He's the son of the lady who cleans our house once a week. Kind of like a godson to us. He's in his last year at the San Luis Obispo Institute of Law. It isn't Harvard. Hell, to tell you the truth, it isn't even Yale. But Clyde is number one in his class and smart as a whip.

Then I played my hole card. "Janet Mason gave us a $15,000 retainer." I hadn't given Karen the check this afternoon. I kept it in my office and stared at it. I think I kissed it once or twice.

Karen keeps our books among other things. I knew it would impress her. It did. She whistled.

"That's great."

"There's only one thing a little peculiar," I said. "She wants me to represent someone else in stopping the development. Susie Wilson." Susie runs the best hair salon in town.

"Why?"

"Ms. Mason thinks the matter shouldn't be in her name."

"I get that, I think." She had a puzzled look on her face. "But why would she want to stop the development? It's part of the community estate. She'll lose half the money."

"Nope. She has a pre-nup. She gets $100,000 a year for ten years."

"Can't you break it?"

I rolled over towards her and propped my head up on my hand. I gave her a knowing smile. "Maybe. But she said Guy was thorough. Seems like our Janet is Mr. Mason's fourth wife."

"That sounds expensive."

"Janet had a lawyer and everything. But Guy selected him and paid the bill. I may be able to attack his independence."

"But if you can break the pre-nuptial agreement, Janet's shooting herself in the foot by challenging the development."

"I told her that. But she says the development's not worth anything until they get the entitlements and Guy will cheat her out of it anyway. She seems a tad bitter. Unlike you, I might add."

Karen wrinkled her nose up and gave me a kiss that redirected the conversation for both of us.

Chapter 3

The business district of San Buenasera is three blocks long and one street wide. Mismatched one-story buildings, fading into the sunset. Funky is the term that comes to mind. The nice term.

San Buenasera was founded in the mid-1800s by spiritualists so the faithful could worship by the sea. Lots of little houses on small lots. The train ran through the middle of town so the faithful could arrive in droves. Which they did.

The town was taken over by hippies in the '60s and had a pretty notorious reputation. We've calmed down. Up until now, the developers haven't discovered us. We like it that way.

I was sitting in a back booth at the Lilly Pad, where the locals go to breakfast. It's a good thing the food is better than Lilly Weston's sense of humor. Lilly's big on frog décor.

I looked particularly spiffy in my pressed jeans, pearl

button cowboy shirt and black snakeskin boots, if I do say so myself. I would have worn my cowboy hat too if I could have found it. And it looked like it was going to rain. Darn.

I eat out a lot. Karen does many things well. I mean really well. But she doesn't do windows. Or cook. Sometimes she reheats. But her good qualities exceed her lapses, far more so than do mine.

It was 9:30. I was picking at my breakfast of fruit and yogurt. I don't like yogurt. I'm not crazy about fruit either. But I need to lose a few pounds. I always need to lose a few pounds. So I avoid eating things I like. Call it the Jimmy Diet.

I had a cup of coffee in front of me. The radio was playing a rousing rendition of "Jingle Bells". Did you know "Jingle Bells" was written by J.Pierpont Morgan's uncle? Maybe the jingle wasn't in the bells. He wrote it in Savannah, Georgia yet. I told you, there was no snow in Bethlehem.

Susie Wilson made her usual grand entrance at the front door of the Lilly Pad and headed straight for my booth.

Susie's an unrepentant hippie. Long skirt, fringed vest, tie-dyed tee shirt, dark straight hair down her back, no bra. Rumor has it she doesn't even charge for sex. If I ever want a joint, I know where to go. And she's not bad looking for a woman in her 50's. She runs a great hair salon.

"Hey, big boy," she said, slipping down into the seat across from me. It's a running joke between us since I'm only 5'7". Or at least I think it's a joke. I stayed at Susie's place for a month about three years ago when Karen kicked me out.

It's not what you think. Susie has an upstairs room over the salon she rents out. But she was around a lot and who knows what she saw.

"How's my lawyer this morning? Ready to take on those big, bad developers?" I hate bubbly this early. I told you, I'm not a morning person. I smiled at Susie anyway. I like her.

"You bet, Susie. We'll rip 'em to shreds."

Lilly wandered over. "Morning, Susie. You want anything?"

Susie looked up. "Just coffee, Lilly. I ate breakfast hours ago."

My God, do people really get up in the middle of the night? I've lived my life on the simple rule that 7 o'clock comes once a day in the evening. Lilly returned with a cup of coffee for Susie. "Enjoy."

Susie lifted the cup and sipped timidly. She made a face and set the cup back down. I pushed my bowl of fruit towards her and pointed with my fork. "Want a bite?" Susie wisely shook her head.

"Tell me how you got involved in this development thing?" I asked.

"Janet Mason gave me $5,000 to do it."

"How do you know Janet Mason?"

"I do her hair. Have since her husband bought that big farm outside of town and moved her in. Or maybe out. She's not a happy camper, Jimmy."

"I gathered. Why doesn't she go to San Luis or Santa Barbara to get her hair done?"

"How about because I do great work." She stuck out her lower lip in an exaggerated pout. I've never seen a woman put her hand on her hip sitting down.

"Come on Susie, you know what I mean."

"Oh, I guess so." She flopped her hands on the table. "I do her hair for half-price."

"Why? Because she's an actress?"

"Yeah, it helps the shop. Maybe. And DSG was my favorite show."

"DSG?"

"'Desperate Shop Girls'. But that's not why."

"Okay, I'll bite."

"She asked. And I'm not the only one. She's done it all over town. She's a real hondler." Susie used to have a Jewish boy friend. A "hondler" negotiates everything. "Janet really knows how to stretch a nickel. You can't even see the buffalo."

That didn't make any sense. Janet Mason parted with a $15,000 retainer easily enough, aside from the usual client grousing. Guy Mason was rich, right?

"What about the $5,000 she gave you?"

"That was a little funny. She didn't even try to bargain with me. Shit, I would have done it for nothing if she'd asked. I hate the way developers are trying to ruin this place. I'm a member of SOC."

"Let me guess. Save Our Community."

"Save our Coast. But you were close. That's what I wanted to talk to you about. I want you to speak up for SOC too when you appear before the City Council."

"Sure. You're the boss. I'll add them to the representation. It might even help." No harm done, right? Right.

Chapter 4

Susie Wilson glanced at her watch. "Oh gosh, it's after ten. I've got to run. Appointment". And she tore off, leaving me and my fruit bowl alone with each other. I tossed in the napkin.

I figured it was time to learn a little more about my client, Ms. Mason and her soon to be ex-husband, Guy. Gee, I sound just like a detective. Using my well-honed skills and two index fingers, I intended to Google them just as soon as I got to my office.

The office is five blocks downhill from Lilly's and a block over. Across the railroad tracks. We're on the wrong side of the tracks. Which, on the Central coast, is the right side of the tracks. Never mind, its complicated.

I thought I could make it. Even without the car. Karen took it this morning when she went to work. Without even asking. Just because the car's in her name. I ask you.

Okay, I'd walk. I'd been practicing walking downhill in

every spare moment. I gritted my teeth and moved out.

I was right about the rain. A fine mist started falling as I left the front door of the Lilly Pad. I tugged up my collar and started to quick step. I forgot to take the umbrella Karen had left by the door. Neither rain, nor sleet, nor snow, nor dark of night . . .

Google, on the stock exchange, is valued at more than Yahoo and eBay combined, and for my money it's worth it. Not that I own any stocks.

I had 600 hits on hubby and thousands on Ms. Mason. "Desperate Shop Girls" was big. Really, really, big. I do lead a sheltered life.

Getting hits on Google is one thing. Reading them is another. I settled in for the duration. If you have the attention span of an eight-year old, the duration can take a while. Before I started to read I called Clyde.

"Yaou sir, bossman. Clyde plays up being black.

"I'd like you to run a Lexis search on Guy Mason and his companies."

"You want me to include Mason Development, Guy Mason Construction and his real estate company?"

Christ, did everybody know who Guy Mason was, but me? "Yeah, just the federal and state courts in Southern

California. Any lawsuits. Maybe for the last 5 years."

"I should do Delaware too. That's where his companies are incorporated."

"Okay. As soon as you can." I told you Clyde was smart.

"I'm shufflin' off to do it right now, boss."

"And Clyde, can the Negro stuff."

"Sho'nuff."

It was getting dark when I finished. It had stopped raining. I had some interesting material. I arranged the papers and my notes along with Clyde's 42-page Lexis search and put them into a briefcase so I could look them over at home before dinner.

Karen offered me a ride. I graciously accepted. We stopped at our local grocery store to buy a roast chicken and all the fixings. Bruno greeted us at the door. His tail was wagging furiously. He's always a lot friendlier when food is at hand. Smart dog.

Karen, Bruno and I were at the table. Karen and I were sitting in chairs. Bruno sat on the floor. Karen was drinking red wine. I had a bottle of non-alcoholic beer. Bruno didn't have anything. We don't let him drink. He's too young.

The carcass of our recently departed chicken sat on the plate. I had wanted to give Bruno the drumstick. Karen wouldn't let me. She cut him up a nice portion of breast meat and dipped it in a little gravy and set it on the floor. Bruno scarfed it down in a heartbeat.

The dog has no table manners. That's why we don't let him eat at the table. But then again, Karen doesn't always let me eat at the table either. When I come back in my next life, I want to be Karen's dog.

I had cleared the table and was standing by the sink holding the dishtowel. That's my job. I clear and dry, Karen reheats and washes. We make the bed together. So far it's worked out okay.

"So what were all those papers you were looking at?"

"I figured I should find out some more about Ms. Mason and her mate."

"So?"

"Interesting. This guy, Mason is Donald Trump without the pompadour. Flamboyant, rich, self-promoting. And I can see why Janet Mason is upset. He's linked in the gossip

That's when my wife, Karen, suggested we move someplace less stressful. Maybe she did a wee bit more than suggest it. I've had many arguments with Karen over the years and I'm proud to say I've almost always had the last word. It's usually "Yes, dear." She has a strong personality. And that's how we came to live in San Buenasera seven years ago.

"Don't give me that, Jerry. You've canceled the last three deposition dates."

You wonder why I hate lawyers.

"No, I don't care about courtesy between lawyers. Get her into a deposition. Put some pressure on her. She'll settle."

Good lord, if the man only worked as hard on my matters.

"No, Jerry, not when you come back from vacation. I don't care about your vacation. I can't take a vacation. If they pull my malpractice insurance I won't be able to pay you."

That hit him where it hurts.

"Okay, that's better." I leaned back in my chair and swung from side to side. I had my eyes closed. Jerry was giving me a headache.

The bad news here is that I'm a really good client of Jerry's. I think I'm just unlucky. Take this case for example.

It was a matter of petophilia. No, that's not a misspelling. We live in a farming community.

You see, this lady owned a small farm and she had six or seven sheep. One got sick and she called the vet. She left him alone and when she came back . . . You don't really want to know. Let's just say the guy's favorite song was "Only Ewe".

So she hires me to sue the vet for emotional distress. To her and the sheep. I bring the suit. It comes to trial. How am I supposed to know the expert I hire can't tell a sheep from a sheep dog? The jury defenses us. The jury foreman's laughing so hard he can't read the verdict for five minutes. So, she sues me for malpractice. See, bad luck.

I hang up with Jerry. It's been a long day. And it's only 10:30. I need a drink. I can't have one. But I need one.

I gave a weary sigh and stretched my arms out over my head. Bruno, who has been asleep on the couch, opened one eye. Nope, not missing anything.

He rubbed his muzzle with one paw and yawned. I yawned. He went back to sleep. Dumb animals.

I can't think of anything else, so I figure maybe I should see what Clyde has come up with on what we need to do to challenge Guy Mason's development of Franklin Farms.

"Okay, let's see if I've got it straight," I said. Clyde gave me a wary nod, his eyes open a little wider than normal. Everyone's a comedian.

"We have to exhaust our administrative remedies. So I have to go before the City Council and lay out the issues. If they approve the entitlements to build all those homes anyway, we file for a Petition for a Writ of Mandamus in the Superior Court. The writ orders the City to follow the law. Assuming we win."

"You got that right, boss."

"Don't call me boss."

"Okay, boss."

I wasn't winning with Clyde either. But Clyde's a good kid. He's had a hard life. He grew up in South Central. His mother got concerned when he started sporting gang colors. Then he got shot. So five years ago she tossed it all in the car, including him, and moved up here. It's the only place along the coast where you can still rent a house cheap. Clyde's mom has guts.

Anyway, we hired her to clean for us, me and Karen. Or is it I and Karen? Well, whatever. This 20-year-old kid was always moping around. One day Karen gets into a discussion with him. The next thing I know he's following me around the office asking all kinds of questions. I realize the kid's really bright. A logical mind. I tell Karen. Karen nods and gives me that "I know" look.

Clyde's got a high school diploma, but no college. So-so grades. We checked into it and the local law school will take him if he's over 21. He takes the LSAT, that's the Law School Aptitude Test, and scores 650. I only scored 595. He applies and gets in.

The deal is, we hire Clyde as our paralegal while he's in school so he can afford to pay tuition and buy books. I thought it was charity. But Clyde's the best thing to happen to this office since we installed the telephone.

"I've looked at what the City Council has to review," Clyde said. "Seems to me like our best bet is infrastructure issues and CEQA."

"CEQA?"

"The California Environmental Quality Act."

I knew that. I was only testing Clyde.

"So, tell me."

"Well, a few things. If Mason develops that place, he's going to be putting a lot of people on the roads 'round here. And water's a big issue with the farmers. They're always complaining there's never enough and it all goes to the city folk. We can also challenge Guy Mason's plans when we see them. And he needs to do an environmental impact report or get a negative declaration. I don't think they can get a categorical exemption from what I read."

"They've got a lot of money and they'll have a slew of experts."

"Shoot, they're building homes for rich folk. Ocean view and all that. We got the moral high ground here." Clyde tapped his finger on my desk.

Right, the moral high ground. I really don't know the terrain, so I'll have to watch my step. I think it might be a long fall.

"So what do you think our strategy should be, Clyde?"

"Delay. I figure we don't need to win. If we hold 'em up long enough, they lose."

Good plan. Particularly the "not having to win" part. That I like. I can procrastinate with the best of them.

So here I am, about to go once more into the breach, chin held high. Just the right angle for someone to give it a good smack.

Chapter 6

"Can you believe it!" Lilly Weston was livid. We're in the back booth at the Lilly Pad. She's got her elbow down on the table, hanging on to a mug in her hand and gesturing with it. Coffee's sloshing around. I'm staring at the mug to make sure I can get out of the way.

"A Starbucks. Jimmy, they're going to open a God damn Starbucks in San Buenasera. Where next? My bedroom? First a bagel bakery and now a Starbucks."

To tell you the truth, I like the bagel bakery. They bake a mean jalapeno cheese bagel. Bruno likes it too.

The Lilly Pad was at its noisy best. The two part- time waitresses were scurrying around with plates of eggs and pancakes stacked up their arms or with a coffee pot in their hands. We were leaning towards each other to hear.

Besides being the proprietor and protectoress of the Lilly Pad, Lilly's an ardent environmentalist. That's why I wanted to speak to her. I figured she was the most likely councilman – uh, councilperson -- to be on my side about the Franklin Farms project. You know, I wanted to kind of line up her vote. She had other subjects for discussion.

"Lilly, what's the big deal? They aren't going to put you out of business. Everyone will still come here for your waffles."

"It's not that. It's the principle of the thing."

"That's kind of why I came over."

"What, you don't like Starbucks either? I didn't even think you knew about it." She opened her eyes up and gave me a puzzled look.

"I didn't. I mean, that's not what I meant."

"Jimmy, you're not making any sense. I mean even less sense than usual." She pursed her lips.

The good thing about living in a small town is that you know everyone. The bad thing is that everyone knows you.

"Lilly, let me start all over. Have you heard about this new development they're talking about up at Franklin Farms?"

"Yeah, I heard a little something. The mayor mentioned it to me. He thinks it's swell." She put her coffee mug back down on the table. Thank goodness. I relaxed a little.

"What do you think?"

She stirred a little puddle of coffee around on the table top with her finger tip. "I don't know much about it. We could use the tax base." She stopped stirring and grabbed the coffee mug. My senses went on high alert in case she started swinging it again.

"Lilly, they've got 1400 acres. They're talking about hundreds, maybe thousands of houses. High priced homes. All kinds of Hollywood types. It'll change the entire character of San Buenasera. Starbucks is nothing compared to what we'll be getting."

"I kind of see what you mean." It gave her pause. I could see her imaging San Buenasera overrun with a Gucci store and a Victoria's Secret. I fired my other barrel.

"What about water. Are we going onto the state water system? You know how we all felt about that. The cost. The price of water. Every farmer within the city limits is going to be on your back." I can be a great orator when I get going. "And all those cars. My God, the pollution."

I left her to think about that. The coffee mug hung limply in her hand. A few more drips of coffee from the side of the mug splashed on the table top.

I made my way down Main Street to see Randy Polivnacov, another one of our sterling councilmen. Every one calls him Polly. Polly's a good guy and not too hung up on legality. I figured I could have an off-the-record conversation and feel him out. Maybe even get his vote.

I wasn't exactly walking. It was raining so I was more or less flitting from doorway to doorway. I forgot to take the umbrella Karen left out for me again. A big car splashed by in the street. Spray wet my boots. I scowled in the direction of the receding car and raised my fist. The guy flipped me the bird.

Polly's store is about two blocks from the Lilly Pad. One thing about San Buenasera. You can get a lot done in one morning.

Polly is our local pornographer. Maybe I overstate. Polly owns the only adult book and toy store in town –- Pussy Galore. Polly's a big Ian Fleming fan. Hey, I can't help it if there aren't more civic-minded people here in San Buenasera who want to serve on our City Council. Besides, Polly can muster a lot of votes. Particularly from the men-folk. I think I may have voted for him myself in the last election.

Polly's window is a crowd stopper. A perfect replica of a 12" phallus. Looks familiar. The sign in front of it says "battery operated and guaranteed shockproof." That's a relief.

There's also an optional strap-on belt. I'm still trying to figure that one out. Maybe you can.

I ducked into the doorway and opened the door. "Polly?" I shouted. Two or three heads popped up from behind the book racks and popped back down again as quickly. I thought I saw the pastor from our local church and our school principal. I'm sure I was mistaken. Polly scurried out from behind a curtain in the back, waving his finger and shushing me as he came.

"For God's sake Jimmy, quit shouting. This place is a sanctuary. You know, like a temple."

An interesting point of view. I'd have to think about that.

Chapter 7

"Nine, eight, seven –- the ball is just about there –- two, one. Happy New Year!!"

I switched off the television set. I can only stand so much ebullience. Karen and I kissed and clinked glasses. Mine was Martinelli's. December 22nd vintage.

"Will you marry me?" I figured it was a good time to ask. We had a fire going. The crackling wood made the room cozy. Rain pattered on the roof. Karen had had two glasses of champagne. That usually makes her a pushover.

"You old romantic," she said.

"I prefer to be called mature," I said. I took her hand and kissed her palm.

She smiled and brushed the back of her hand over my cheek. She laid her head on my chest and put her arm around me and squeezed.

"No," she said.

"No? How can you say no? Not even maybe? Come on. Give a guy a break. It's New Year's Eve." I was working on a look of righteous indignation. I think I need more practice. She giggled.

"Okay," she said, stifling her giggles. "Maybe. Want to make love? I'll make it worth your while. It was nine o'clock. I forgot to mention that we were doing New Year's Eve on New York time. San Buenasera isn't the liveliest place on earth.

"It's going to be an interesting New Year," I said. I was awake, which is unusual for me after I suffer *le petit mort*.

"Umm." Karen stretched languorously and tugged the covers up under her chin.

"They've scheduled the City Council meeting on the Franklin Farms project for January 28th."

"Uh-huh." Karen pulled the covers up over her head. Was she trying to tell me something?

We were having breakfast at the Lilly Pad. Bruno was lying at Karen's feet, snoring. He'd had a hard day on Sunday sitting on my lap and watching the football games. The Lilly Pad makes a Health Department exception for Bruno. I don't know if the Health Department knows about it.

It was a holiday. I didn't see any reason why we had to close the office on the day after New Year's, just because New Year's fell on Sunday. But Karen disagreed. She won. Big surprise.

She was having her usual breakfast of dry toast and hot water. She treats herself by putting lemon in the water. Yummy. Karen weighs 110 pounds, so she has to watch her weight.

I was having coffee. I was hung over from all the Bowl games. That's the reason I was also having a waffle with fresh bananas and maple syrup. A guy's got to treat himself when he has a hangover. Everyone knows that.

"Didn't you say the City Council had scheduled a meeting to consider the Franklin Farms project?" She was holding her cup in both hands and looking at me over the rim.

"I didn't think you were listening."

"I was. I just wasn't talking. What happened to my romantic?"

"You wouldn't marry me." I gave her my petulant look.

"But I did fuck your socks off." I love it when Karen talks dirty. It's a treat she doles out impishly.

She gave me a big white-toothed grin. Her green eyes sparkled. I could see the gold flecks.

Great. My barber was John D. Rockerfeller. John D. ran a comb through my hair and patted it into place.

"You seen that big gray Mercedes around town?" Sal asked, removing the paper clerical collar from around my neck. He dusted on some talcum powder. "No hair spray, right?

"No." A big car around town, other than one just passing through, was news. Particularly a Mercedes. The locals drove mostly old Toyotas with tattered political bumper stickers. "Is it Janet Mason's car?" I said.

"The television star? Nah. She drives a little BMW. Green."

Sal's an authority on the pedigree of expensive foreign cars. He might have a lot of money stashed away. Maybe I could start billing him.

"Besides, this car belongs to a guy. Slick looking. Rides around in back. Driver's an ugly dude." Sal whipped off the barber's cloth and snapped it smartly.

"Look's good." He handed me a mirror so I could admire his art. He twirled the chair around so I could see the creeping bald spot in back. Sal isn't Mr. Sensitive.

"What do you know about this guy in the Mercedes," I said. "Is he buying a place in town?" Not another developer. What was San Buenasera coming to?

"Nope. Bert says he's not stayin' at any of the hotels." The nice hotels are outside of town, strung up along the coast. Bert is Sal's brother. He services all the hotels around here. "And Andy says he ain't heard of a guy in a gray Mercedes looking around." Andy is Sal's cousin in the real estate business. Sal has a big family.

"If you hear anything, let me know. I'm interested."

"Yeah. I heard you're representing Susie in opposing that Franklin Farms development." So much for privacy. "Don't much like your chances the way I figure it. But that's okay."

"Why. You don't want the town to change, do you?"

"Don't know. Could be good for business."

So much for my local support.

Chapter 9

"LouAnne, you look good. I had slipped my binoculars into my desk. I don't think she noticed. "Teaching must agree with you," I said.

LouAnne Jenkins teaches third grade in our local elementary school. She's a pretty good-looking woman of maybe 35. I wish my teacher looked like LouAnne when I was in third grade. Brunette. Nice legs. Not that I noticed. I'm almost married, as I've explained.

I was always an "A" student in monogamy. Even with my first wife. 98%'s an "A" in anyone's book. Anyway, I was glad for the interruption. A new young lady had been bouncing around topless on the sloop in the harbor. I love California. But I was beginning to have lascivious thoughts.

I had gotten LouAnne a divorce from Calvin Jenkins about four years ago. I had counseled her to try to make the marriage work. But she was dead-set on a divorce, you should forgive the pun. You see, Calvin owns our town's one and only funeral home and cemetery.

She said she couldn't take any more raucous funeral directors' conventions. And besides, she couldn't stand to ride around in the hearse anymore. I had always thought it was kind of colorful.

"I have to have the child support agreement amended. I can't raise Charlie on what I'm getting. Not with prices being what they are." She was sitting in my client chair, hair in a neat bun, knees primly together, her red handbag grasped in both hands and held securely on her lap.

She was ignoring Bruno who was watching alertly from the couch. That was surprising. He was usually asleep. I thought he might have something useful to add. I gave him an inquisitive look. He didn't.

"What do we base a modification request on?" I asked.

"I don't understand." She grabbed her handbag tighter and pulled it in.

"The court originally set the alimony and child support based on Calvin's income." A freight train lumbered by. I held up my hand to LouAnne and grimaced. The train blasts its horn at each railroad crossing through town. It stopped my brilliant legal analysis cold.

I started again. "We can allege greater need, and it helps that we're talking about supporting Charlie, but that's the tough way to go. It would be better if we can show there's more money."

"Oh, I see. I think Calvin's doing well. I heard he's buying another funeral home in Arroyo Grande."

"Great. Maybe Calvin won't object to the modification. If we can do this without going to court it would be better for everyone."

She started laughing. She put her hand over her mouth but her shoulders were shaking. I noticed her hands were rough and her fingers were unmanicured. Third grade's hard work.

"What's so funny?"

"Calvin's the cheapest man who ever walked the earth. Don't you remember?" Actually I didn't.

She stopped to catch her breath and started to laugh again. I thought it was a little hysterical. She finally got hold of herself.

"Will he object? You can bet on it," she said. "When we were married he used to make me wash Charlie's drinking straws, so he could use them again. Calvin would pinch a dime so hard that it wouldn't just scream, it would die straight away."

"Well, it's worth a shot. Maybe I'll go over to the funeral home and talk to him."

"Sure, if you want to. But I don't think it will do any good."

I didn't really want to go over and see Calvin. One of the problems I've had as a trial lawyer is I hate confrontation. So, I don't like going to court. Maybe I should have received more job counseling before choosing a career. Anyway, seeing Calvin was the right thing to do. And I didn't think it was going to be a problem.

When you're handling a divorce or custody case, it's smart to know something about the spouse. More than one attorney has been shot or beaten up by an irate husband. Yeah, I know, I'm no Adonis, but Calvin is Mr. Milquetoast by comparison. I wasn't concerned.

Not like it had been in L.A. I used to have a criminal practice. Dope dealers mostly. They paid well and it was all in cash. Easy money. Until a case went sour and some of my client's friends didn't like the way I had handled the matter.

They started making threats. I never told Karen. I didn't want to scare her. But some of those threats were directed at her too. It scared the hell out of me. That's when I started drinking.

When it was all over, I promised myself that I wouldn't ever put her or me in that position again. I have a nice, low key civil law practice up here in San Buenasera. I intend to keep it that way.

I was on my way over to the funeral home to chat with Calvin when I saw the big gray Mercedes that Sal had told me about turn onto Main Street from under the freeway. The funny thing is, the only place that road goes is up to Franklin Farms.

Chapter 10

It was a dark and balmy night. Dead winter on the Central Coast. Have I mentioned I love California?

Our City Hall is a converted 1930's office building about three doors down from the "Pussy Galore". What our city lacks in character, we make up for in color.

A crowd of people was milling around and chattering outside the doors of the City Council chamber, waiting for the meeting to start. Sandals were the shoes of choice. And beards were de rigueur. For the men, I mean. Mostly. There was a distinct smell of pot that pervaded the assemblage. Karen and I were on the other side of the crowd.

Clyde, our paralegal, is a rugged looking guy and he cleans up well. Some people think he cleans up better than me, but they're wrong. I know that because Karen once told me when I felt insecure. There are some things in life you have to cling to.

Clyde was wearing pressed chinos and a blue turtle neck

sweater under a blue cashmere blazer with horn buttons. He looked like a stud and Janet Mason was standing right beside him. Very close.

City Hall rocks on the nights our Council meets. It's the best entertainment in San Buenasera and it's free. It's usually a hoot. Our little community has more than its share of kooks. And every one of them has something to say. Depending on the evening's prior level of substance abuse, some of those comments can be – unusual.

Guy Mason and his entourage swept in around 7:45 and he started introducing himself around the crowd. His tailored sports clothes had just the right touch of informality. His barber did a great job with the little hair he had to work with. Mason looked a little out of shape under the fancy duds. But this guy could have run for political office. I would have voted for him. He was smooth.

Mason spotted Janet standing next to our young black man. He leaned over and whispered something to a man who had come in with him and started over towards her. My eyes met Karen's, rehearsing what was to come. She gave me the whisper of a smile.

We were too far away to hear what was said, but Mason bent down and gave Janet a kiss on the cheek. I was holding hands with Karen and leaning nonchalantly against the wall.

Mason turned to Clyde and held out his hand. Clyde took it and said a few words to him. He held on.

Then he reached into his jacket with his other hand and handed Mason some papers folded lengthwise. Clyde smiled, gave Guy Mason's hand another shake and stepped back. That's when the shit hit the fan.

My mother once told me that a gentleman doesn't shout "What the fuck?" in a crowded room. I guess Guy Mason wasn't a gentleman. Some people just get upset when they're served with a divorce summons. Who knew?

The assembled multitude stilled instantly as the red-faced Mr. Mason threw a hay-maker at our boy wonder. Clyde stepped inside the punch and delivered two short jabs to Mr. Mason's belly. He dropped like a sack of potatoes. Clyde turned and ushered Janet Mason away as Guy's entourage rushed towards him.

As they came by us, Janet nodded to me, a broad, unpleasant smile on her face. She wasn't beautiful. My client was beginning to make me think that the word "woman" was a contraction of "woe man". I shouldn't have such thoughts. I promise to be good in the future.

I guess a little summons, delivered with panache, can ruin your whole day and maybe even your presentation before the City Council. As I was developing that thought, the doors swung open and people started to enter the Council chambers.

That's when Mr. Mason delivered a surprise of his own. There were only three Councilmen on the dais. Lilly Weston and Polly Polivnacov were no where to be seen. And three is still a quorum.

"What the fuck?" I said. To my credit, I said it in a whisper and I didn't try to hit anybody. Mom still wouldn't have approved. I took one of the agendas that were being handed out at the door.

"We're last on the agenda. We're going to get screwed. They want to hear this when everyone else has gone home," I said. Sometimes I'm so insightful it scares me.

"Gentlemen. I'm James Emerson Harris. Everyone knew me, but there are the formalities. "I'm here representing Susan Wilson and Save Our Coast." Good start. It went downhill from there.

"But you can't . . .," I said.

"But we have . . .," they replied.

"But the traffic impact . . .," I said.

". . . tax base to improve the roads . . .," they said.

"But water . . .," I said.

"We have an environmental impact report . . .," they concluded.

"Prepared by Mason Development experts," I said.

"Tough titty," they said. That's not what they actually said, but that's what they meant. That was just before they approved the development plan for Franklin Farms by a two to one vote and threw us ever so politely out of the room.

"That didn't go as well as you hoped," Karen said. Karen has a knack for understatement. "But you sure stuck it to Guy Mason –- right before he stuck it to us. I wonder what happened to Polly and Lilly?"

I was wondering more about what had just happened to me.

Chapter 11

I was sitting in my office, staring out over the harbor. Mulling over how I had been outmaneuvered. I was so distracted I didn't even have my binoculars out. The small, choppy waves flashed in the muted winter sunlight. My mind was as empty as the top of my desk.

Bruno, on the other hand was cool. Then again, he didn't have my problems. He stopped licking his paws and hopped down off the couch, eying me to see if I had a free lap. I waved him away. "Not now, boy."

He made a small noise in his throat. Bruno has mastered the hurt-dog look that can instill more guilt than my Catholic mother. I surrendered. I don't have much backbone.

Lilly Weston had resurfaced the day after the Council meeting. 24-hour flu. I believed her, of course. Even if she had trouble meeting my eyes. And Polly returned to town a few days later. He had a sudden emergency with his mother in Florida. I didn't even know Polly had a mother. Come to think of it, maybe he doesn't.

I believe in coincidence. Just not too much. It was all too convenient. I banged on the desktop with my fist. It hurt. I'll have to remember not to do that again. Bruno ignored me and shifted in my lap to a more comfortable position.

Damn it, I should have won at the City Council. This is my turf. I know the rules. Or at least I thought I did. Maybe I was dealing here with something bigger than I assumed. In lawyer talk, "assume" means it makes an ass of you and me. They got that one right. I had been handed mine.

I was just reaching for my binoculars when Guy Mason burst into the room. I rent a small house and it's only about four steps between the front door and my office. Guy was dressed today in a beautifully tailored woven black silk blazer over a black tee shirt. His beige linen pants look like he never sat down. I think I was in love.

But it's embarrassing to be caught with one hand on your binoculars and a dog in your lap. People are so suspicious.

"Who the fuck do you think you are?" He had his fists balled up. Guy can't seem to speak in a normal voice. Maybe it comes from being a developer.

I put the binoculars down and rummaged around in my right hand desk drawer. I found a business card. I held it up about six inches in front of my nose.

"It says here I'm James Emerson Harris. That sounds right."

He was flummoxed for a moment, but he recovered quickly. "You're nothing but a drunk and a hack, you little prick." His face wasn't a pretty shade of red.

I hate compound statements. They're so difficult to respond to. Besides, he'd never seen me naked.

"No," I said. "But I appreciate your pointing it out. Can I get you a Diet Coke?" Always be nice to people who are shouting at you. It confuses them.

That stopped him for a moment.

"No?" I said sweetly.

He regrouped.

"What do you think you're doing?" he said.

Wow, now we were getting somewhere. Maybe he could tell me.

"You don't have any idea what you're getting into." He pounded his hand on my desk. If he'd asked, I would have told him that wasn't a good idea. "I'm going to bury you."

"Yes," I said. Would you like to sit down?" I waved towards my only client chair.

"You're a fucking idiot," he said, as he turned and walked out.

I wanted to stop him. He hadn't told me what I was doing. I could use the help. But, I resisted. Too proud I guess. I just wish I knew whether he was complaining about the divorce action or the development. Then I could know when to be scared. It would have eased my mind.

So what was I going to do? File a lawsuit on the land entitlements, of course. That would certainly make me popular with the City Council. I'd have to get more money from Janet Mason. I raised my hand and pointed upwards with my index finger. Ah, I'd discovered the silver lining here. And besides, I'd get to see if she was as penny-pinching as Susie Wilson had said. That still didn't make sense to me.

The trip up to Franklin Farms took maybe five minutes. Janet had seemed a bit reluctant when I called. But she agreed when I explained not filing a lawsuit would delay our screwing up the grant of entitlements to her husband. Nice lady, Janet.

Janet was in a skimpy bikini with a little transparent covering over it. It didn't leave much to the imagination. She was in a lounge chair in the backyard by the pool. I reminded myself that beauty is only skin deep. But I've always known that skinny-dipping had its amusements. I banished the thought from my mind.

"You certainly screwed up the Council hearing," she said right off.

Not a good opening when you want to ask for more money. "I got sand-bagged." Maybe I sounded a little bit petulant. "It won't happen again." I hoped. "We've made our administrative record. We need to file a lawsuit. Mason won't be able to get financing if we're challenging the entitlements. It'll stop him dead in his tracks for at least a year."

She liked that. Her smile was the same one the little boy had when he was riding the tiger.

"But, I need another $20,000." I waited.

The silence hung around like a drunk at a bar.

"That's a lot of money," she finally said.

"It's a lot of work."

She stared at me. Then she nodded and stood up. "Stay here." It was the same tone I bet she used with the maid.

She came out after a couple of minutes with a thick envelope. It had 200 one hundred-dollar bills in it. I hadn't seen a hundred-dollar bill since my days defending drug dealers. I was beginning to like Ms. Mason in spite of myself.

As I was leaving I looked back towards the far end of the house. The rear of a gray Mercedes was just poking out.

Chapter 12

"She really gave you $20,000 in cash?"

"Yeah, she did." I passed her the envelope.

She lifted the flap. Her short red hair trembled as she shook her head in disbelief.

Karen and I were at Mario's, a little Italian restaurant we like in Arroyo Grande. She was in jeans. I, on the other hand, looked natty in my sports coat and tie. They're reserved for clients and court.

Mario's is a local's place tucked back away from the highway. Checkered tablecloths and candles. I love to look into Karen's eyes in the flickering candlelight. Tonight her delicate features blended into the shadows with a flash of white teeth as she spoke. Fetching. She always looks fetching when she's holding an envelope with $20,000 in it. Outside it was starting to drizzle again. Inside it was getting toasty. It bode well for my future.

It wasn't every day I got a $20,000 fee. I wanted to

celebrate. Clyde had dropped Karen off on his way home. I got to drive the car today. It's a classic Jaguar. I bought it in happier times. I love that car. Even when it doesn't run. Which is often.

I had a court appearance in San Luis after my visit with Janet Mason. On the 20-mile drive back to meet Karen, I found myself ruminating about Ms. Mason. Karen and I had rented the fifth and final season of "Desperate Shop Girls" the other day and we had spent a thrilling evening with the ladies assembled. I didn't even bill Janet for the time. I should have.

My first impression was that Janet Mason was either the best actress I'd ever seen or the worst. That may confuse you. It reminded me of something that one of my professors did in law school. He wrote on the board, "The king can do no wrong." Then he asked us what it meant. Trick question. Trick question. They're doing that all the time in law school. Well, it meant either the king was above the law so he couldn't do anything wrong or it meant that if the king did something wrong, he could be punished under the law. I know my professor was getting at something. I'm not sure what.

That's how it was with Janet Mason. As far as I was concerned, the role she played on "Desperate Shop Girls" was Janet Mason in the flesh. A true bitch goddess. On the other hand, if Janet was acting the role for my benefit, she was the greatest actress I'd ever seen. Somehow, I doubted it. Besides, according to the trades, she was the only actress on the show who was never nominated for an Emmy.

So, what was this all about? This divorce was going to shaft her financially. I couldn't imagine Janet enjoying that. I had spoken to her about the possibility of setting aside the pre-nuptial agreement and she seemed to be attentive, but not all that interested. I would have thought it would be the most interesting subject in the whole world.

And why was she so willing to come up with the money for the lawsuit to challenge the City Council? In cash yet. She didn't make a big scene about it, which is what I would have expected from any other client. Who had that kind of cash lying around? And if she did have that kind of cash, why was she hondling all the merchants in town for a discount? I guess you have to be smarter than I am to figure it out. I was going to ask Bruno the first chance I got.

The food at Mario's is good. It's also cheap. Usually that's a prime recommendation for me. I was proud we didn't turn our back on an old friend just because we now had money. The fact that Mario was letting me run a tab had absolutely nothing to do with it. I intend to pay him some day. I'll even give him a discount the next time someone challenges his liquor license.

I was sipping an O'Doul's. Karen had a glass of Zager Chardonnay. She lifted it to me. "My hero." The smile that illuminated her face melted my heart.

I gave Karen my best boyish grin and raised my glass with a modest nod. Karen tucked the envelope into her purse. I knew I'd never see it again, which is probably all for the best.

Maria, Mario's wife came over. "Buorgiorno. Iss good to see you." She elongates her s's. A little Italian ancestry maybe. She was born in Italy. That might have something to do with it.

Maria is round and jolly. She takes care of the front of the house. Mario does the cooking. "Tonight, you should have the veal. It is beautiful."

"How are things, Maria? Business good?" The place was full. Midweek yet. "Soon, you won't have room for us."

"For you, always. But last week we have a movie star. This week, I don't know."

"Who?" I could guess.

"This famous television person. One of my most favorite shows. Janet Sullivan. She very beautiful." Ms. Mason's stage name. "And the man she was with." She raised two fingers to her lips and kissed the air.

Funny, I wouldn't describe Guy Mason that way. Well dressed, maybe. Rich. "What did he look like?"

"Tall. Dark curly hair. So Italian. I think about dumping Mario." She tittered.

Now what?

Chapter 13

Comes now Jimmy, knight-errant, with his pen for a lance. Accompanied by his faithful page, Clyde. Picture colorful banners snapping in the breeze with family crests rampant. The sound of trumpets echoing in the air.

Hold on. After watching the final episode of "Desperate Shop Girls" last week and noting the current state of thinking in the world, I feel obligated to assure you that all the talk of homosexuality in the Middle Ages was greatly exaggerated. Just so we're all on the same page here.

I'm speaking of going into battle for the fair Janet or Susie or SOC. I'm an attorney. I've humbly bent the knee of fealty to my lord client. I've attorned. Get it? Attorney, attorned. Oh, and I got $20,000. Maybe there's more where that came from.

So, it's Wednesday. Clyde and I and Bruno are sitting in my office. Bruno's sitting on me. Perhaps sitting is a euphemism. The sun is puddling on Bruno who is stretched out across my lap, snoring. Hardest working dog I ever saw.

"I reviewed the draft Petition for Writ of Mandate," I said. "It looks pretty good. Where here do we file it?" I ask this questions because I like to make Clyde feel important.

"Superior Court. San Luis."

"Do you see any problem with including Save Our Coast?" "Nope." Clyde raised his head from rereading a paragraph in the draft. "Actually, I think it'll help. It gives the Writ more gravitas." He tapped on the Writ with his forefinger.

Clyde talks funny. I have to hold him down.

"Besides," he said, "Susie asked us to. She's the client."

"You'll take care of serving the city?"

"Yep. Soon as we file."

"Oh, don't forget. We have to serve Mason Development."

Clyde shook his head and crocked an eyebrow at me. "I'm glad you thought of that," he said. I thought there was a touch of humor in his voice. That's what I get for being on top of things.

"How about Ms. Mason's divorce? What are we doing?"

"I prepared the notice of Guy Mason's deposition and the subpoena for his financial records. I put them on your desk yesterday." He pointed to a pile of papers on the corner of my desk that I had successfully ignored for a whole day.

I cleared my throat. "Okay, let's get them out."

"You don't want to look at them first? Make those subtle changes that make them great documents."

"Just send them." Jeez.

"What do you think we should do about Clarence Jenkins?" he asked.

My discussion with Clarence, the undertaker, hadn't gone as well as I had hoped. As a matter of fact, when I mentioned paying more child support, he got all red in the face and squeaked at me, in a threatening kind of way. Have you ever been attacked by a rabbit? Let me tell you, it isn't pleasant.

"LouAnne Jenkins has got to get us a retainer. I hope she has some money." I didn't want to do this for a reduced fee again. It would be bad for my tough-guy image. After all, I was now a big-time entertainment attorney. "Then we'll file to amend the child support decree. Why don't you get to work on that if nothing else is pressing."

"Okay, boss."

That's what I like. Respect. "Don't call me boss."

"Sorry, boss. It won't happen again." Clyde got up and left. He missed all the fun.

I got out my binoculars and turned my chair carefully to the window. I didn't want to disturb Bruno at his work. I looked out over the harbor. My eyebrows did a Groucho. I think my mouth fell open.

Gosh. There were two girls on the boat today. Naked as the day they were born. Real hard-bodies. And what's that they're doing? Then, the phone rang, damn it. I turned and punched the speaker button. Bruno opened one eye.

"Jimmy Harris." I said, swinging back to the window. I still had the binoculars glued to my face.

"Mr. Harris?"

"Yes."

"Can you hold for Mr. Guy Mason?"

"Sure." It was probably one of the few calls that would make me lower my binoculars. I'll forever wonder at what happened next out there.

"Mr. Harris?" It was a man's voice.

"Right here."

"This is Guy Mason."

"Hi."

"Hello. I just called to apologize for the scene I made in your office the other day. I was out of place. I owe you a drink."

"I appreciate the apology. No drink called for."

"I insist. Can we meet somewhere this afternoon?"

I have to admit I was intrigued. This was not the Guy Mason I knew and loved. "Of course. How about here in my office?"

"I'm in San Luis today. What about the bar at The Seashore in Shell Beach. 5 o'clock."

"I'll be there." I said. You bet.

Chapter 14

It gets dark around 5:30 in the winter. The sunsets are glorious. Sometimes there's a green flash at the horizon when the sun finally drops into the ocean. It's a sight to see. And the bar at The Seashore Lodge is the place to see it. Romantic. Although I wouldn't suggest you do it with Guy Mason.

I was about 10 minutes late. An accident on the 101. Guy Mason was sitting at a table by the window when I came into the bar. He rose and extended a ham hock of a hand.

"Jimmy. May I call you Jimmy?" He gave me a toothsome smile. Definitely sincere. I'm sensitive to these things.

"Sure." I took his hand. "Sorry I'm late, Mr. Mason. Accident . . ."

He interrupted. "Hey, no problem. Glad you could make it. Call me Guyboy. All my friends do."

Friends? Guyboy? I sat down at the table trying to figure out if I could get my mouth around "Guyboy".

Guyboy sat down and brushed at his well-cut sports coat. It looked like cashmere. I once heard a TV person comment at one of those "trials of the century" that the room was full of lawyers in $1000 suits. I think Guyboy was wearing two of them. And it was only a jacket.

"What'll you have to drink?"

"An O'Douls."

"Oh, yeah. You have that drinking problem thing. Lot's of my friends have that."

I was glad to know I was in the good company of Guyboy's friends.

He signaled the waiter who appeared as if yanked by a string. Boy, I wish I could learn that trick. Breeding, I guess.

"An O'Doul's. And another one of these." He pointed at the short thick glass on the table in front of him and pushed it towards the waiter. Judging by the color in his cheeks, he hadn't waited for me to start.

"So, Guyboy," I said. It didn't fit right in my mouth.

"Jimmy, I really did want to apologize to you. I mean about the City Council and the other day. I like the way you handle yourself. Shows class and poise."

Finally, someone who understood me. God was smiling.

"You know a man in my business is always looking out for people who know how to handle themselves. That little stunt you pulled on me at the Council meeting was real clever. Something I might do."

Actually, did, if I recalled properly. I gave him my boyish grin and a modest nod. "Thanks, Guyboy."

"So, I wanted to see if you'd like to be on my legal team."

"Sounds interesting. What'd you have in mind?" I sounded like the accounting guys who audited Enron's books when they were asked how much is 2+2.

The waiter brought over the O'Doul's and a thick glass filled with a brown liquid I assumed wasn't Sarsaparilla. "Can I get you anything else, sir?" Guyboy shooed him away. He reached over and scooped up a handful of nuts from the little dish on the table and popped them in his mouth.

When he stopped chewing he leaned in closer to me. "Look, this Franklin Farms thing is going to be a huge project." He spoke in almost a whisper so I was leaning in too. Some flakes of chewed nuts landed on my sleeve.

"A thousand sales. We need a good lawyer on the spot to handle all the legal questions and do the legal work on the sales contracts. It'll be years. And after that we'll have this San Luis project I was up here on."

"Wow." I'm so verbal. I flicked at my sleeve.

"What do you charge?"

I hesitated. Usually that's a question I would hasten to answer. I must be losing it. "Gosh, Guyboy. I'd love to be on the team. I really would. But I'm suing you. I have what we call a conflict."

He brushed that aside with a wave of his hand as if it was a pesky fly. "The big boys deal with conflicts all the time. I know entertainment lawyers down in LA who're representing the studio, the actor, the producer and the bank. If you're going to play in the big time, like we're talking about, it's something you'll learn to deal with."

It was an interesting outlook. I could live with that, I thought. "But, Guyboy, I'm suing you for divorce." I mean, it wasn't the movies.

"Oh, that." He made it sound like it had slipped his mind. "Shoot, I'm a grownup. You go right ahead. Be doing me a favor, really. Janet's a roaring bitch." He paused. "Funny, she was never that way before we got married." He paused again and regained his momentum. "Besides, I've got a real good pre-nup." I could have enlightened him, but I didn't think that's where I wanted to go.

"If you would consider it, I could put you on retainer right now," he said. I cocked my best eyebrow. He passed a thick envelope across the table. "I thought $100,000 was about right. Of course, that's the minimum, against your time." Funny how you can see environmental issues in a new light when you're talking to a knowledgeable man.

"Let me think it over," I said. I didn't touch the envelope. I knew myself well enough to avoid temptation. I can resist anything except temptation. I took a drink of my non-beer to keep from blabbing out how I would take the job. I can't be bought. But I can be rented.

"There's just one thing." Guyboy said it with a big smile. How could it be a problem? "The Franklin Farms project. We have some unusual financing on that. We need for it to move along. So we can get it done and pay off everyone. And so you can get to work. That objection stuff you were talking about at the City Council meeting was right dumb, if you don't mind my saying so." I allowed that I didn't. "I really think it should go away. Don't you?"

I gave him a nod and sipped at my O'Doul's.

Chapter 15

We were lying in a post-sexual haze. The cowboy hat that Karen had been wearing was now covering a strategic part of her body. She's always been sensitive about that right foot of hers. I wish I could twirl a cowboy hat like that.

I was breathing hard. Karen was grinning up at the full moon crowding into the room with us through the sliding glass doors. Bruno was sleeping in another part of the house. I mean I couldn't see him sleeping. But I know Bruno.

I think it was my cooking that turned her on. When I got back from Shell Beach, I whipped up a pot of my famous spaghetti. Topped with Ragu sauce, it creates lust. Thank the Lord.

She wrinkled her nose and rolled over. The cowboy hat went sailing onto the floor. She curled up around me and made a purring sound deep in her throat. Her red muff made a nice warm spot against my thigh.

"Will you marry me?" I said. Take advantage of them when they're down.

"Maybe," she said.

Damn. Missed again.

"What are you going to do about Guy Mason's offer?" Her voice was muffled against my chest.

"I heard about this Chicago judge," I said. She shifted position and looked up at me. "He returned $10,000 to an attorney who was trying a case in front of him. One of the attorneys had given him $10,000 and the other had given him $20,000. He wanted the bribes to be the equal so he could decide the case on the merits. Maybe I could just take $35,000 from Guyboy until all the matters are resolved."

She punched me in the shoulder. "Be serious."

"Oh. Serious."

"Yes."

"Okay. Serious." I sat up and leaned back against the headboard. I turned towards her. She had her head propped up on a bent elbow, waiting expectantly. "I think Mr. Guyboy doesn't give a damn about the divorce. But he cares a lot about the Franklin Farms project. Enough to give me a whopping bribe to get me off his back. It made me feel kind of good actually."

"Why?"

"Well, two things. It feels nice to be worth that kind of money to someone." I was hoping for a better offer. Karen resisted the temptation.

"And." She raised her head off her hand to look into my baby blues.

"It told me a lot about our case. He really doesn't want to be delayed. I'd say he's terrified of being delayed."

"Can you delay him that much?"

"I figure for at least a year or two. It'll cost him a fortune."

"Really?"

"Yeah, it'll take six months for this case to be tried in Superior Court. Briefs and all. That's if I can't stretch it out and I probably can. Then, the judge will take it under submission. It could be a few months before he decides. After that, if we don't win, we can appeal. Who knows how long that will take."

"Don't you have to put up a bond?" Karen rolled over and sat up.

"Nope. Not under CEQA." I got my head into a more comfortable position on the headboard.

"CEQA?"

"Damn, it's cold in here," I said. "I seem to have lost my heating pad." She smirked at me. Women are so unkind. I scooted down under the blanket. She got under too. She nudged me with her elbow.

"The California Environmental Quality Act. CEQA."

"How do you know all this?"

"I'm smart."

"I'll bet Clyde figured it out."

"Don't be such a smart ass, woman or I'll beat you." That scared her.

She rolled towards me and put up two little fists in front of her. She said, "Oh, yeah."

I would have fought with her, but I thought she could take me. She went quiet for a minute and her green eyes lost their focus. A sure sign that she was putting something together.

"Doesn't the State want all kinds of housing built?" she said.

"Absolutely."

"How does CEQA help?"

"It doesn't."

"Does that make any sense?"

"Not to me. But it's not for me to reason why. It's for me but to do and collect my fees."

"I'm glad you're not taking his money."

"Hey, I'm a highly ethical attorney. Besides, I forgot to tell Guyboy that Clyde had already filed the Petition for Writ of Mandate before we had our drink."

"What do you think Guy Mason will do when you tell him?"

"Not a thing. What can he do?"

You can't be right all the time, even if you're a great lawyer.

Chapter 16

The next week was really dull. Nothing was happening at the office. The sloop in the harbor was bereft of even one pretty young thing, much less two. Even Bruno was bored, and that takes some doing. I kept thinking about that envelope stuffed with $100,000. I had to slap at my hand to keep from reaching for the ghost of it.

Guyboy had been less than pleased when I told him I couldn't serve, but only stand and wait. He had been quiet. Even though I was really nice. I told him how I'd be pleased to represent him after the existing two matters were resolved. I knew how much he needed me. He just muttered something about how I was going to regret my decision. Heck, I already did.

I was singing a little song to myself and tapping on my desk with the end of a pencil. I had just about concluded I shouldn't give up my day job when the intercom buzzed. Pamela, our receptionist-assistant whispered something.

"What? Talk louder." She whispered something else. She

sounded out of breath. "I can't hear you. What's wrong?" The intercom went dead.

I was gathering myself to get up to find out what was going on when Pamela flew through the door. You have to understand. Pamela is a very nice young lady. And she can type very well. But she's about 5' tall and weighs around 200 pounds. She doesn't fly. Never.

Her face was flushed. "Do you know who's in the lobby?"

"No. To tell you the truth, I was hoping you would share that with me."

"Andrea Gann." Andrea Gann's a reporter for the CBS station in LA. It has the hottest news show on the West Coast. "She's got . . . got a cameraman with her. They taped me." As if it were an unusual occurrence in our office. I would have to speak to Pamela. Just as soon as I could get my wits about me. "She wants to speak to you."

Well, of course.

"Paul, move a little to the right." Andrea Gann motioned him over a couple of feet with her hand. "I don't want the water in this shot." The cameraman took two steps towards the window.

She turned to me and held out her small manicured hand. The fingernails were blood red and we hadn't even started. I should have known.

"Mr. Harris. I'm Andrea Gann." She had kind of Asian-American good looks. I took her hand. She had a firm grip for a small woman. Something was niggling at me. Something I'd read. It might have been helpful if I'd remembered at the time. I recalled it about two days later, when it was far less useful. I'd seen her name linked to Guy Mason's when I'd Googled him.

"Don't you usually call for an appointment?" I said. She had caught me in my old flannel shirt and jeans. It's comfortable. But she definitely had me beat by a mile, fashionwise.

"This is a scoop. You're representing Janet Sullivan in her divorce. Correct?" She was using Janet's stage name. I nodded. It was my, "I'm hot shit" nod.

"How'd you find out about the divorce?" I said.

"We're a major news organization. We have our sources." She had such a nice sweet voice.

"How can I help you?"

"Mr. Harris, just sit down behind your desk. Look at me and not at the camera."

Her dark straight hair matched her good looks, if not her name. And she smelled nice. She had piercing dark eyes. I blush to admit I'm a TV virgin. Pamela and Karen were loitering in the background, whispering. Bruno just looked curious. I think he was hoping Andrea Gann would feed him.

She motioned for the cameraman to start recording. He nodded at her. Her voice became emphatic.

"There have been rumors that Janet Sullivan has been seeing Gino Bartoletti?" she said. "Does that have anything to do with this divorce filing?"

She took me by surprise. Who the hell was Gino Bartoletti? "I'm sorry, that's a matter of attorney-client privilege. I can't comment." I'm pretty good at making it up as I go along. How was I to know that according to KCBS I had just refused to comment on the rumors that Janet Sullivan-Mason was having a relationship with Gino Bartoletti, the head of the United Union Pension Fund. Identified by the FBI as a known associate of the Gambrella crime family. I don't think that's what I said.

"Isn't it unusual to have a major Hollywood personality file for divorce in such a small, out-of the way place? Does she want to keep this a secret?"

I shrugged. "Well, she lives here. It makes sense."

"Of course. She hasn't worked since "Desperate Shop Girls", has she?

"I wouldn't know." Again with the wrong answer.

"But aren't the best divorce attorneys in Los Angeles? You aren't a divorce specialist. Why did she choose you?"

"We do pretty well up here too." I gave her my patented smile. She seemed markedly unimpressed.

"You don't have a lot of experience with high profile cases do you, Mr. Harris?"

"I've handled my share." I'm sure I didn't sound defensive. I'm a master of self-control. And I didn't say share of what. But the way this was going, it wasn't going to generate a lot of client referrals.

She looked around the office. "It appears you don't have much of a practice." I guess she's not a fan of minimalist design. I ordered Bruno to bite her. He just sat there looking at me. He's not well attuned to my mental commands. Darn.

She leaned in closer and the corner of her red lips twitched. "Didn't you have a problem with the Bar Association a few years ago?"

"Nothing much." I shifted in my chair.

"Weren't you publicly reproved in a client theft scandal?"

I don't care how it looked on television. I'm a master of the poker face. I bet they digitally altered my expression.

Chapter 17

Gino Bartoletti is a nice man. Or, at least, that's how I see it. After all, he didn't break my legs. Maybe he didn't want to tangle with a celebrity lawyer.

I was sitting in a booth in the Lilly Pad about a week after my interview with KCBS when this big gray Mercedes pulls up outside. Out steps a tall, trim, dark complexioned guy with curly black hair. He was dressed in dark slacks and a black cashmere turtleneck sweater under a soft, black Italian leather jacket. The guy who let him out of the car was dressed as a fireplug. If fireplugs come in XXXL. I'm glad Bruno was with Karen. Bruno has an unfortunate predilection for fireplugs.

Heads turned as Gino crossed the Lilly Pad, heading towards me in the back. Hey, I'm not jealous just because he's a good-looking guy. A pretty young thing once told me I was suave and debonair. At least I think she did. We were having dinner when she said it. She pronounced the phrase "swave and deboner." I thought then she was referring to the physical state of the front of my trousers, but thinking back on it, I realized de boner was under de table at de time.

Gino seemed to know who I was. He sat down in the booth across from me without asking. I put down the mug of coffee I had been sipping at.

The fireplug stepped to one side, his huge hands clasped in front of him. There was a notable bulge under his left arm. He stood staring at the front door, his back to us.

Gino didn't say hello or hold out his hand. He stared at me for a moment. His eyes were the darkest brown I have ever seen. A moment can be a very long time. I had a strange problem with my throat. The edge of my lip twitched. I think it was trying to smile.

A waitresses scurried over.

"A double decaf cappuccino, please." Gino gave her a brilliant look. Thank God, he could talk.

"Uh, sir. We don't have cappuccino." She made it sound like she would have killed to avoid the inconvenience she was causing him. "Could I get you some decaf coffee?"

He looked up at her. I thought she was going to swoon.

"Sure." I'd never heard the word said with such passion. "Would you like anything else? We make wonderful waffles."

"No. Thank you." So polite.

"Can I bring something for your friend?" She made a small motion with her head towards the fireplug.

"No. He doesn't want anything." The fireplug didn't move.

She hurried into an excited murmur with the other waitress. She kept casting her eyes back over her shoulder at Gino and smiling. And to think, I come in here all the time and she'd managed to restrain herself.

Gino turned his deep brown eyes on me. Up close you could see that his nose had been broken. He spoke very softly. I found myself leaning forward to hear him.

"You shouldn't embarrass me, Mr. Harris. It's not good manners." He had my undivided attention. "And I demand good manners from people I do business with."

Wow, a lot of information. We were doing business. I allowed as how I wouldn't want to cause him a problem for all the cattle in Texas and I was sorry if I did. And could I just go flagellate myself. I've raised groveling to a high art.

The waitress returned with the decaf coffee and set it in front of him.

"Thank you." His eyes never left me. "I don't like my name on television or in the newspapers." He had very big white teeth. All the better to eat you with, I'm sure.

I'm not very brave. I wanted to scream "It wasn't me. It wasn't me. It was that awful Andrea Gann." but he continued on before I could get it out.

"From now on, I'd like you not to give any more interviews. Just do your job."

He left me there nodding my head like a bobble doll. He never touched his coffee. Or me, for which I'm grateful.

Chapter 18

My office phone rang. I like that. It makes me feel wanted. I reached over for it.

I'd been a good boy since Mr. Bartoletti favored me with his views. I'd not given a single interview. And if this was the press, relentlessly hounding the famous celebrity attorney, I was prepared to defer with vigor. Fortunately for them, it wasn't.

"James Harris," I said. My voice has depth and timbre. One might even venture mellifluous.

"Mr. Harris?"

"Yes."

"John Campion here.

"Hi."

"Do you know who I am?" His voice radiated confidence.

Of course I knew who he was. Campion & Gilbert was the most powerful law firm in L.A.

"No," I said. No use giving him a swelled head. "Oh. Uh -- I'm an attorney in Los Angeles. We're representing Mr. Guy Mason in his divorce and in connection with the Franklin Farms project."

"Great. What can I do for you?" I try to be chipper when dealing with my colleagues at the bar.

"I was hoping you'd consider an extension on our delivery of the financial information you requested from Mr. Mason."

"I'd like to accommodate you Mr. Campion, but I have instructions from Ms. Mason to proceed without delay." I'd have to remember to have her give me those instructions the next time I talked to her.

"Mr. -- errr." I heard him shuffling some papers. "Harris, you do know that Mr. Mason has a pre-nuptial agreement."

"Sure. We're challenging it on the basis of failure of representation."

"That's a long shot."

"Maybe. We don't think so." I leaned back in my desk chair and crossed my legs. I tapped my fingers on my knee and waited.

His voice turned more truculent. It was just a question of time. "You know, we can go to court and have your discovery request postponed until after your motion to set aside the pre-nuptial agreement is heard. That's a lot of trouble for both of us."

Actually, less for me. I'm here. Mr. Campion is there. See, nothing escapes me.

"Mr. Campion. I'm sure the courts down in L.A. are ferocious in protecting the rights of distressed husbands. Up here, they're a little kinder and gentler."

He sighed into the phone. "You do know we have a very large firm." I was pleased for him and said so. "I'll have a motion to continue on your desk in the morning," he said. I ventured as how I couldn't wait. We get so little excitement up here.

I was sure he would have a motion on my desk tomorrow. I only hoped I'd be able to lift it.

The line went quiet. I could almost see Mr. Campion taking off his reading glasses and tossing them on to his desk. I've always wanted to do that. It looks so cool. Silence rolled down the line and filled up the room.

"I also see you're handling a matter challenging the entitlements for the Franklin Farms project," he finally said.

"Yes."

"Isn't that a conflict with Mrs. Mason's divorce matter?"

"Yes." He wasn't going to get by me with any of his trick questions.

"Well?"

"Well, what?" I unfolded myself and leaned forward. I held the telephone a little bit away from my ear. I think I was annoying our Mr. Campion just a tad.

"Are we going to also have to move to have you barred from handling one or both of these matters?" No more play nice with Jimmy, I guess. Mr. Campion must have had a deprived childhood.

"Actually, I don't think so."

"Oh?" He sounded incredulous.

"I have conflict waivers."

"Written?"

"Sure."

"I see. Would you mind sending them to me?"

"Of course not," I said. Just as soon as I got them. I'm not always as straight forward as one might hope.

"Clyde," I shouted as I hung up the phone.

Home is where the hearth is and the hearth in this case is only a few blocks up the hill. Good commute. I had just told her about my conversation with John Campion. Karen was impressed. Which is good because we were laying naked in bed. Or at least I was laying. Karen was sitting up against the backboard. Bruno was sleeping on the floor.

"Guy Mason has trotted out the big guns," Karen said.

"Yeah, it looks that way. Campion & Gilbert has 350 lawyers last time I checked." I made a face. "I expect they'll try to bury us in paper."

"What are you going to do?" She put her hand against my cheek. I got a warm and mushy feeling.

I smiled into her delicious eyes. "Me. Nothing." Dramatic pause. "But Clyde may have to stay up late. It'll do the boy good. Develop stamina and all."

She tittered. I like making her laugh. It kind of melts me inside.

Karen went quiet for a moment. "Have you figured out what Gino Bartoletti meant by your doing business with him?"

"No. I was hoping you had." Karen's deep. I live most of my life out loud.

She shook her head and her hair shimmered in the moonlight coming in over her shoulder.

"I'm pretty clear about one thing though," I said.

"Umm."

"Better with him than against him." Mama didn't raise no dumb children.

She settled into my arms, her small naked breasts pressing into my chest. I moved my right hand down and to the left and changed the subject.

Chapter 19

Rain was tinkling all over the windows in my office. It was as gloomy as the inside of a coat closet. I know, because that's where Clyde found me. I sometimes catch a nap in there.

You have to be really cool when you're awakened on your closet floor. I yawned and made my way back to my desk. Clyde and I were now locked in discussion. I was more rested.

"Why'd it take so long?"

"Boss, these things just take time." He shrugged to let me know he respected me deeply for asking.

Clyde had just handed me the conflict waiver from Save Our Coast that John Campion had been hounding me for. I'm a really creative guy. But the "dog ate it" wasn't going to fly much longer. I'd already given him the ones from Janet Mason and Susie Wilson. You'd think two would be enough. Some people are never satisfied.

"And don't call me boss."

"Right, boss."

"So, what took so long?"

"Susie got it."

"Okay." It was a quizzical okay.

"She just gave it to me."

"I figured that. I didn't think you were sleeping with it." Sometimes I think Clyde likes to play dumb. I can be dumber. I don't find it all that difficult.

"SOC is going through some kind of reorganization. Susie had a problem getting someone to sign it."

Finally, I squeezed it out of him. The great lawyer at work. "Do me a favor and fax it to John Campion."

He stood up to leave. I motioned him back down.

"How're you doing on the response to his motion?"

True to his word, Mr. Campion had delivered his motion to delay discovery the day after our pleasant conversation. I couldn't lift it. Clyde and I had hauled it into his office together so he could work on our response.

"They use a lot of words."

"Any you don't understand?"

"Nope. But I'm pretty sure Judge Anderson won't understand a few." Judge Anderson had been assigned to hear the motion. She wasn't the strongest peg in our judicial coat rack. But, on the other hand, she'd been an outstanding fundraiser for our local state senator before she got appointed to the bench. "You going to explain them?"

"Thought I'd let those smart city boys do that."

"Good idea."

Bruno seemed to agree. He opened one eye, yawned and rubbed his nose with a paw. A sure sign. You just need to know what to look for.

"When do you think you'll have something for me to look at?"

"Maybe later today."

To be fair to Clyde, I was frustrated. It had been raining for three straight days and there wasn't a soul on the deck of any boat in the harbor. I had even resorted to doing some legal work.

"Let's try to get the hearing for the Jenkins motion to modify her child support set up for the same day as the Campion motion. That way I can double-bill the time."

Clyde raised an eyebrow.

"Don't look at me like that. You're my apprentice. I'm trying to teach you the subtleties of practicing law."

"Oh, swell. You think I can come watch you in court?"

"Sure. It'll do you good to see a master at work."

Clyde seemed duly impressed. Or maybe he just fell asleep.

Then he said it. "Indians."

"Bless you," I responded.

"No, Indians. You know, Native Americans."

"I think they died out around here a long time ago."

"That's the point," he said.

"Of course." I wasn't about to let on that I had no idea what we were discussing. Besides, it was kind of interesting in a non-specific sort of way.

"We want to delay the Franklin Farms project, right."

"Uh huh."

"Indians."

His argument seemed circular. I pointed that out to him as gently as I could.

"The Chumash used to be all over the place along the Central Coast," he said.

Still were. I know. I'd lost money in their casino. Mucho wampum.

"Why don't we call the State and request an archeological survey of the Franklin Farms property?"

"Now that's a good idea. It'll give us another string to our bow." See how I get into the spirit of things. "And given our State bureaucracy, it'll take them three years to figure out where the property is. I think we're on to something."

I used "we" because I wanted Clyde to feel included. I don't like to take all the credit. It isn't good for morale.

"Why don't you go ahead and call the State. Maybe you can also schedule the motions. And you better co-ordinate with Janet Mason and LouAnne Jenkins. In the meantime, I'll work on my oral argument." Actually, I was looking forward to going back into the closet and continuing my nap. I sure had Clyde fooled.

Chapter 20

It was 6 a.m. I was hopping up and down on one stockinged foot in the semidarkness of our bedroom, trying to get the other foot into my pants. Thank goodness I'm better at getting into Karen's.

The lady in question was making a soft rising and falling lump in the blankets. A certain long-haired dachshund was snuggled up against her. Bruno was suspiciously quick at taking my place. I was considering having him followed.

It was raining, as usual. Downright gloomy. But a brilliant lawyer is undeterred.

Today was show time. Motions to be argued and decisions to be made. If the Jaguar would start and didn't break down on the way to court. The car was beautiful. It was a woman in a car's body. I could usually get her fired up. But she was unpredictable over the distance. Particularly in the rain. Among other minor faults, her windows leaked. Usually down my sleeve, no matter where I put my arm.

I was getting an early start so I could swing by and pick up Clyde. He had done a great job on our papers. I thought we were in good shape on the discovery motion. But Clarence Jenkins had been a surprise. The attack rabbit was fighting us on the child support like his life depended on it. Not good form for an undertaker. I grabbed my blue tie and my one and only sports coat and padded out of the room holding my shoes in my hand.

The Superior Court in and for the County of San Luis Obispo, Department 6, the Honorable Sandra J. Anderson presiding. A temple of justice if I've ever seen one.

Janet Mason was front row, right. Guy Mason was front left. A full cast. Gino Bartoletti sat in the back of the courtroom with his legs crossed, watching. I nodded at Mr. Bartoletti as I came in. He ignored me. I was glad.

I stopped half way up the aisle. Sitting next to Guy Mason was John Campion of Campion & Gilbert. That seemed weird. John Campion must charge $1000/hour. To argue a discovery motion? Against me? In a podunk court in the middle of nowhere?

"All rise."

And then I was up to bat. "May it please the court," I said. It rarely had before, but hope springs eternal.

My oral argument was brilliant. Everyone said so. Or they would have if I'd taken a poll. I sat down.

John Campion rose to his full 6'2" and came to the bar. His blue pinstriped suit fit as if it had been made for him. Duh. Three of his myrmidons leaned eagerly forward in their chairs to absorb every suited word the master might utter. Their pens were poised over legal pads emblazoned with the name of the law firm.

Clyde had taken in my every word as well, but up here we're more laid back. Clyde had had his eyes closed. I intended to quiz him on the way home in the car.

Campion gave Judge Sandy a brilliant smile. I think he has his teeth whitened. It took ten minutes for my vision to clear.

Sandy Anderson ascended to her present lofty judicial position from the divorce bar, among whom she was know affectionately as the "Barracuda". Three times married and now three times divorced, she was comfortably fixed financially. Mr. Campion might not have known all that as he lifted his hand and opened his mouth.

"But, your honor . . ." Campion shook his beautifully coiffed mane of dark hair with the famous gray streak in front. "I don't think . . ."

He gesticulated. His delicate manicured hands danced a ballet in the air. His resonant voice filled the stage.

"But you can't . . ."

But she could. Not only that. She did. Mr. Guy Mason had thirty days to produce the financial records we had requested. Bang.

The courtroom cleared like a dance hall after someone shouted "Fire". As Guy Mason walked out, I saw Gino Bartiletto lean in towards him and whisper something in his ear. Mason drew back and shook his head violently. His face paled.

I have no idea what that was about. I didn't even know they knew each other. How did that fit in with Gino Bartoletti's remark about doing business with me? What the heck was going on?

I didn't have a lot of time to muse on the question. The Jenkins' child support motion was up next. LuAnne couldn't come. She had to teach. But the attack rabbit was there in full menace.

I presented our case. Clarence Jenkins' lawyer told a tale of losses and capital required. It almost broke my heart. Sandy Anderson took the matter under submission. As I turned, Clarence Jenkins caught my eye. If looks could kill.

Wow. I was making a lot of friends lately. And our town wasn't that big.

Clyde and I made a detour to check on a case scheduled for another court. I was chatting with him as we pushed through the doors to the parking lot. He put his hand on my arm to stop me. I looked up.

"I think we got a problem," he said. He was right, as usual. The Jaguar was listing to the left, looking like a beleaguered ship that might go down at any moment.

As we walked over to the car I noticed a hearse pulling out of the courthouse parking lot. The rain wet the bottom of my trousers as I stared down at the two flat tires into which someone had stuck an ice pick.

Chapter 21

The sun was out and Bruno and I were back in business. We were doing our business with a pair of binoculars rampant. Cute pink nipples paraded atop firm proud breasts. We were cheering them on. It was too good to last.

The two days following the hearing had been quiet almost to the point of snoring. I could live with that.

The phone rang. This was becoming chaotic. Maybe I should have it taken out. Or at least get an unlisted number. If this kept up, I'd be working full time. What would Bruno do?

I waited for four rings. Maybe they'd give up. No such luck. I sighed and lowered the binoculars. I took my boots off the windowsill and swung around towards the phone. Bruno held on for dear life. I picked up the receiver.

"Mr. Harris?"

"Right on," I said.

"Hello."

"Hello to you. Who is this?"

"Sorry. This is John Campion."

Oh goody. "What's up?"

"I wanted to congratulate you on your presentation the other day. I was impressed. You certainly beat the socks off us."

"It's nice of you to call, John." I'm getting cynical in my old age. I'll bet that's not why John called. "Can I call you John?"

"Sure. I'll call you James."

"Jimmy actually."

"Excellent. Jimmy, I wanted to ask your help. We often need local representation on the Central Coast. I wanted to speak to you about becoming our co-counsel in matters requiring local representation on the Central Coast. You showed us the value of local knowledge."

Was this Guyboy redux. John Campion wasn't that dumb.

"That's very flattering. Particularly from a lawyer of your caliber." In my language, caliber measures how big an asshole I'm dealing with. John Campion was definitely high caliber. "Unfortunately, as I told your client, I've got a conflict."

"Well, maybe we can do something about that."

Ah-ha. The carrot and the schtick.

"We're prepared to make a generous settlement offer to Mrs. Mason," he said.

"Please." I'm a man of few words, particularly when someone offers to talk about money. Those few words are always polite. Besides, I wanted to hear what generous was. I rubbed the side of my face. It had started to itch. I get excited easily.

"If Mrs. Mason will agree to dismiss her lawsuit and enter into a voluntary joint dissolution of the marriage and property settlement agreement we will give Mrs. Mason $2,000,000 in addition to paying the $100,000 per year agreed to in the pre-nuptial agreement."

"That is generous." Over the top as a matter of fact. "Cash upon the grant of the divorce?" I looked down at Bruno. He nodded in approval.

"Mr. Mason will have to refinance the Franklin Farms project. Until he can do that, he'll give Mrs. Mason a second trust deed on the land."

"I'll talk to her about your offer. But I still have a conflict. My clients are challenging the Franklin Farms entitlements." I tried to sound sad. Actually, it wasn't too difficult.

"I realize that. I also want to discuss settling that matter."

This was getting interesting. "Shoot."

"Well, your clients want to protect the environment up there. Isn't that so?"

"Right." I wondered where he was going with this.

"What if we agreed to put 800 acres of the 1400 acre property into a land trust and also agreed to only develop 400 homes on the remaining acreage.

There was a deep rumbling sound. "Hold on a second John." There was a train going by. Twice a day. The room shakes when you're just a block from the tracks. So do your fillings. I'll bet this isn't a problem John Campion has to deal with. The noise subsided. "Sorry about that. You were talking about limiting the number of houses."

"Yes. But what was that awful noise?"

"Nothing, John. Go on." I didn't want the conversation to get off track.

"Well, as I was saying, in addition to the donation to the land trust and limiting the housing, we would consider a large contribution, say in the neighborhood of $1,000,000, to a trust for environmental protection to be administered by your clients. The contribution would be made as the homes are sold."

I scratched at my cheek again. Maybe I was allergic to money. That would explain a lot of things. "It's a very interesting proposition. I'll need to speak to my clients, of course." That's when an Indian arrow hit me in the back. Savages.

What was I going to do about the Chumash? Clyde had already called the State to inquire about sending in the archeologists. I hadn't discussed the idea with my client, Susie. It seemed irrelevant. We wanted to stop the project. The thought of a settlement never entered my mind. This could really screw things up. Hold on. It had only been a week or so. Clyde probably hadn't filed the papers. I'd stop him.

John Campion interrupted my thoughts. "Certainly, Jimmy. Get back to me."

"Will do," I said jovially. But I didn't feel it, at least until I could get to Clyde.

"And don't forget about working with us. You might find it very lucrative."

"Not a chance I'd forget, John."

This made no sense at all. I'd won a motion. How important could that be? Yet here was a major law firm waving as big a white flag as I'd ever seen. Boy, I must be good. Obviously that's why John Campion wanted me on his side.

My next call was to Janet Mason. I figured that speaking to Susie was a waste of time until Janet agreed. I didn't see much of an issue. $2,000,000 in addition to the pre-nup amount was excessive. I mean I'm good, but breaking the pre-nup wasn't a sure thing by a long shot. After all, our theory to challenge it was kind of out there. Actually, way out there.

Janet picked up the phone on the first ring. Maybe she thought I was her agent. I gave her the short of it. I'd save the long of it for Karen.

I explained our chances and what we might recover if we succeeded. Even if we succeeded breaking the pre-nup, if Guy Mason had kept his pre-marriage property separate, Janet wouldn't be entitled to any of it under the community property laws.

Besides, my research had indicated that Guy had not been doing that well financially over the last few years. All in all, I recommended to her that we take the offer if we could get some cash up front. Hell, I think I used the word "leap".

Janet listened. Then she laughed. It wasn't a "funny ha-ha" laugh. It was a "scratch the board with your finger nails" laugh. "Fuck the settlement offer."

"Janet, that's not a good idea. Let me go back and see if I can improve on it."

"You damned asshole. Just do your job. I told you. No!" Still sweetness and light, my Janet.

This case was getting stranger and stranger. Nobody was acting like they were supposed to. No one except me. Oh, and that's when I forgot to talk to Clyde about the Indians.

Chapter 22

The Lilly Pad was crowded. This always happens during tourist season. At least after 9. It's the antique shops. That's what they come for.

I was standing at the breakfast bar that stretches across the front window. Tourists don't stand. I had my boot on the bar rail, and I was finishing a waffle topped with strawberries and whipped cream. Don't raise your eyebrows. I'm still on my diet. Everyone knows anything you eat standing up isn't fattening.

I was leafing through the New York Times. I heard a tourist once say the way to tell a good place to live is if you can get the New York Times and a good bagel. Come to think of it, Lilly's bagels come frozen.

Okay, I don't usually read the New York Times. Some thoughtful soul had left it on the breakfast bar. I usually read the San Buenasera Beacon. Obviously the superior news purveyor. But it's one of my cardinal principles of wealth management to never buy a newspaper when I can get one free.

My coffee was cold and I signaled to my friendly waitress and pointed down at my mug. She wandered over with the coffeepot and splashed more coffee into the cup. Then she wandered away. Maybe I should tip more.

Anyway, as I was searching for the comics, an article caught my eye. I took another sip of my coffee as I perused it. Interesting. It seemed the FBI had raided the offices of the United Union Pension Fund and hauled away computers and financial records. The article referred to my new friend, Gino Bartoletti, and his unusual business associates.

I figured that would make him a bit tetchy. I recalled he told me he didn't like publicity. Maybe I would avoid Mr. Bartoletti for a while. That fit right in with my existing game plan. I glanced at my watch and closed the paper. Bruno and I had an appointment.

The two new tires on the Jaguar were performing splendidly. We were on our way back from San Luis Obispo. I was driving. Bruno wanted to, but I nixed that. It was a glorious day on the Central Coast.

Highway 101 parallels the ocean here. The view is great. An Amtrak Surfliner caught up with us and passed on the right. The ocean side. That train along the coast runs on some of the most desirable land in the world. I had always wondered why. So, a while ago, I asked an old farmer in town.

He said sure. That was easy. When the railroad came through in the late 1800's, the coast was mostly farmland. The farmers naturally sold their worst land to the railroad. The least productive. You know, down by the beach. Oh.

The sun was shining. A few fluffy clouds were chasing each other about like sheep at a sex orgy. It must have been 65 degrees. Unfortunately, the electric windows on the Jaguar weren't functioning at the moment or I would have had my arm out. Bruno was sprawled on the passenger seat. I can never get him to wear his seat belt.

We had been to the vet. Or rather, I had taken Bruno to the vet. The vet had given him a shot. Bruno was now looking up at me with those liquid brown eyes as though I had betrayed him.

Neither of us liked the vet. I think it's because Karen once suggested we get the vet to neuter Bruno. He had plopped down on his stomach and looked protective. Damn right. I had empathized completely. We guys have to stick together.

"It wasn't me, Bruno," I said. "It was Karen who said you had to go to the vet." Tell it like it is. Shift the blame. Whatever. "You were sneezing. She was concerned. For all I cared, you could sneeze all over the house. I didn't know he was going to give you a shot."

Bruno looked deep into my eyes. He wasn't buying my story.

I turned to stare at the ocean. I'm a sucker for guilt. It's never too late to blame your mother.

I started thinking about the conversation I had yesterday with John Campion. I promised I would get back to him after speaking with my client. The whole thing still didn't make sense to me. I rubbed my chin and reviewed the conversation in my head.

"I agree, John. It was a generous offer," I said. I had just delivered Janet Mason's message.

"Aren't you even going to make a counter-offer?" Campion asked.

"Nope."

"What do you expect me to do? Negotiate against myself."

"That would be interesting." I changed the phone to the other hand and grabbed my Diet Coke.

Mr. Campion wasn't amused by my humor. He was gruff.

"Shucks, John. You don't have to be so harsh." I took a sip and waited.

Campion screwed himself up to utter his ultimate cut. He accused me of not having client control. I hung my head.

"But I think I may be able to settle the Franklin Farms suit," I said. I was hoping to get back into his good graces. Susie Wilson had been interested. Rightly so. 800 acres is a lot of land to have for green space. An acre is a furlong in length by the distance it takes to turn around a horse and plow. That's about 22 yards. A furlong's an eighth of a mile. Multiply. About 44,000 square feet in all. A little less than a football field. 700 or so football fields in total. More than enough room for fun and games.

He laughed at me. "No way." Campion was dismissive. "The offers were dependent on each other."

At the time I just thought he was being pissy. Actually, I got a little pissy myself. I reminded Mr. Campion that we still hadn't received any of Guy Mason's financial records. He had muttered something that I didn't quite catch. I knew it couldn't have been "Go fuck yourself." A lawyer of Mr. Campion's quality would never have said such a thing. He had hung up rather abruptly. I don't think I bring out the best in people.

But the conversation didn't add up for me as I thought it through. Campion was too much of a professional to let a settlement die because he was angry. Why wouldn't Guy

Mason want to settle the Franklin Farms lawsuit? There was big money in it for him. And risk from not settling.

He had a window of opportunity. Time was money. He'd want to push the development forward as quickly as he could. In his mind it had to be a totally different issue than the divorce. And no one knew Janet was behind the lawsuit. All Guy Mason knew was that I was the attorney in both matters.

It just didn't make sense. Like everything else about this case.

Chapter 23

I was working at my desk, intent on the important issues
of the law with which I occupy myself. I had just leaned
forward to make a note. It was dark and gloomy at 4:30 in
the afternoon. Cloudy, no rain. That's not why I was
working at my desk instead of looking out over the harbor.
I'm a diligent fellow. Bruno was asleep on the sofa, as usual.

It had been four days since my chat with John Campion.
We still hadn't gotten any financial information. If this kept
up for another week, we'd have to file a new motion. Clyde
was going to love that. But at least we had the Jenkins' child
support motion out of the way. The decision had come in
this morning. Another victory for the Jimmy.

The upper window behind me dissolved in a spray of glass
before I heard the crack. I sent my desk chair skittering as I
dived under the desk. Bruno elbowed me aside, the coward.
I was there first. Karen burst through the door.

"Jimmy, Are you all right."

"Get down."

She dropped to the floor and crawled over to join me and Bruno under the desk. It was getting a little crowded. I reached my hand up gingerly and groped for the telephone. Broken glass was all over the top of my desk. I pulled the phone down to join us. Then I called the police. It was a shame to break up such a great party.

Chief Walter Carsone arrived 45 minutes later. That's sounds more impressive than it is. Our police department has five policemen, three of whom are on night duty. The police station is near City Hall, right across from our famous oak tree. History has it the tree was planted by Father Junipero Serra himself on his way through town. Everybody else got a mission.

We had crawled out from under the desk to greet the Chief. Karen was laughing and pointing at my head.

"You look like a party animal with all that glitter in your hair."

I instinctively brushed at it. "Ouch." That was not a good idea.

Chief Carsone is a heavy, slow moving man. He made it a point to meticulously examine the scene of the crime. It took him about six seconds.

"Just some kid with a pellet gun probably. Nothing to worry about." He made a dismissive gesture with his hand.

Chief Carsone wasn't taking our little incident too seriously. That was comforting since he was a highly trained professional. He'd cut his teeth as a policeman in the crime-ridden town of Arroyo Grande. Right down the coast. When he was a patrolman, the town had been beset by a scourge of jaywalking. He was assigned to the task force to stamp it out. It was that success that got him his job as our Chief of Police. That and his relationship to the mayor's wife.

"It didn't sound to me like a pellet gun. It sounded like a rifle." I pointed at the far wall near the ceiling. "And that hole doesn't look like it was made by a pellet gun."

"Those darn pellet guns are getting pretty powerful." He walked over and looked up thoughtfully at the large hole in the wall. His hands were stuck in his back pockets. He turned. "You got termites?" he asked.

"Very funny, Chief."

"Well, Mr. Harris, let me tell you. Someone fired through the top part of that window, and if it was a rifle like you think, it hit the wall up there. Bullet's long gone. If they were looking to hurt you, I think they might have aimed a little lower." He didn't make it sound like it was such a bad idea. Besides, how did I know they weren't just a lousy shot?

It occurred to me that the additional tax revenues from the Franklin Farms development, that I was trying to scotch, would be good for a couple of additional patrolmen and maybe a new car. I know it couldn't have anything to do with the Chief's attitude. I just thought I'd mention it. As I've said, I've made lots of friends in San Buenasera.

When you've got glass in your hair you shampoo with a great deal of care. Thank God Karen was there to comfort me. We were singing in the shower as I went through the rinse cycle.

I don't know what I'd do without Karen. She knows I'm not a hero. I think she puts up with my stupid humor because she knows that's how I cope. I'm a lucky guy.

The next two days we worked at home. At least Bruno and I did. Karen went down to the office. She had windows in her office. It was a little too breezy for me. And there was something about having to turn my back. I wasn't concerned about myself. But Bruno is a sensitive kind of guy.

I was beginning to think someone didn't like me. Now who could that be? I'm such a nice fellow. My tires had been ice-picked. My window had been shot out. I might as well be back in L.A.

I didn't think it was Guy Mason. Guyboy was too smart to do it. Besides, big businessmen don't act like that, do they?

Hadn't I offered to settle the Franklin Farms matter? I still thought he would come to his senses.

Obviously, it wasn't my buddy, Gino. We were doing business together, or so he said. And I didn't think he would aim to miss if he had someone take a shot at me. It wasn't a theory I cared to test.

But someone was trying to tell me something. I was ready to listen. I just needed for them to speak more clearly. Preferably over the telephone.

I figured I should probably call LouAnne Jenkins to find out if Clarence was armed. And to explore his approach to business development. Just call me an old worrywart.

Chapter 24

Tuesdays are always tough. Most people say Mondays. For me it's Tuesdays. Maybe I gear up for Mondays and run out of steam by Tuesday. It's a long week. Who knows? But Bruno feels the same way. We've discussed it.

It was my first day back. Anyway, Clyde popped into my office. "Great to see you, boss." Much too chipper.

I was standing behind my desk. My back was to him. I didn't want to come out and play. I was feeling kind of long-faced. I ran my finger around the edge of the window glass the glazier had replaced. Then I turned and sat down in my desk chair. "How's it going?"

Clyde looked nifty in his green merino wool sweater and pressed jeans. Maybe we were paying him too much money.

He plopped an envelope on my desk. "First financial info in response to our subpoena to Mr. Guy Mason." He had this smug smile looping his lips.

The envelope was about three inches thick. "Doesn't look like much," I said.

"Isn't. About enough to avoid sanctions, I figure. We need to hire an accountant."

"How about Tony Thompson?" Tony Thompson was the accountant who referred Janet Mason to me. Tit for tat.

Now there's a lip-smacking phrase. I've been looking for a tat mine for a long time. Good for bargaining. But alas, the phrase doesn't have anything to do with breasts. It's actually a 16th century expression meaning a tap for a tap.

"Why don't you catalog what we have . . ."

"Done that. Tax returns for four years."

"Not very meaningful. Get them over to Tony. I'll call him and tell him what we need him to do."

"Okay." Clyde gave me a nod.

"And you might draft a letter to Mr. Campion lamenting this paltry response and requesting immediate compliance with the subpoena. You might also hint at a motion for sanctions."

I sighed. This was going to be a long, painful process. But every time we filed a motion, Campion's firm would have to send someone upcountry to appear. We could make it expensive for Guyboy. We just had to be careful not to overdo it and piss off the judge. If I lived long enough, we'd get there. I shuddered as that phrase rattled through my brain. I was sitting with my back to the window.

"Oh, Janet Mason called," Clyde said. "She wants you to call her."

Maybe she'd changed her mind about the settlement. I reached for the telephone as Clyde departed.

"Janet. It's James Harris. What's up?"

"When you called me about the settlement offer, I forgot to ask you something."

Maybe a term of the settlement offer. Maybe she was interested. I settled in with the phone. "Okay."

"Did they mention anything about Franklin Farms?"

That one took me by surprise. "As a matter of fact, they did. They made a very good offer to settle that lawsuit too." I hoped she would notice the "too". She didn't.

"I don't want you to settle it." Meaning the Franklin Farms suit.

That was peculiar. Did she think it gave her leverage? How, since Guy Mason and his attorneys didn't know she was involved. At least I didn't think they did. But they'd made their settlement offers conditional on each other. I was confused. It's not unusual, my being confused, but I usually know why.

I didn't see any reason to break it to Janet that she wasn't the client in the Franklin Farms lawsuit. She was paying the bills, but it was Susie Wilson who was the client. At Janet's request. Since it didn't make any difference, I just said, "Okay " again and left it at that.

"We got the first disclosure on our subpoena," I said. That caught her attention.

She lit up the line. "That's great."

"It's not much. Some old tax returns. We hired Tony Thompson to review them."

"Who cares. I don't give a fuck who you hired." Apparently analysis wasn't on the top of her list. "I want you to push that bastard for all the information."

"We're going to. But discovery can take some time."

"Why?" There was skepticism in her voice. "Do I need a tougher lawyer?"

I switched the phone to my other hand and rubbed my ear. Boy, that wasn't far under the surface. This was a client to love. She was really starting to piss me off. Then I thought about the money I'd gotten and more that was to come. I have my principles.

"Janet, we can't go down there and raid the place." Like the FBI did to your friend Gino, I left unsaid. "All we can do is push and if we don't get the stuff, go to court and ask for sanctions. We may have to do that several times. We'll get it eventually."

"I don't want eventually. I want to get this done now. Are you trying to get more money out of me?"

Well, yes. But not the way she thought. "I can't tell you it won't cost more money." Actually I could, but this didn't seem like the right time. "But, money won't speed this up."

"I don't want to hear that, damn it. Do something." I heard her mutter a phrase about the bedroom habits of lawyers. She slammed down the receiver.

I did something, just like she told me. I reached into my drawer for my binoculars and turned around towards the window. But my heart wasn't in it.

Chapter 25

Janet Mason and Gino Bartoletti were sitting together towards the back of the courtroom. The only lawyer from Campion & Gilbert who showed up for our motion was a tall, thin young man in wire framed glasses who looked like his clothes didn't fit him all that well.

Guy Mason had been unable to locate additional financial information as readily as we had hoped. He must have lousy records. It had permitted John Campion and me to have several more pleasant phone conversations. When he shared with me how difficult it was for Mr. Mason and how hard he was trying, I was moved. So moved, I moved for sanctions. And here we were.

The thin young man was arguing earnestly. I really liked the way he moved his hands for emphasis. And how he whipped off his glasses when he made a big point. It must be a Harvard thing. He'd been on his feet for five minutes. It looked like he was just getting warmed up.

"We've done everything we can. They've asked for so much irrelevant . . ."

Judge Anderson didn't seem all that sympathetic. She gave him the gimlet eye. Then she banged down her gavel. He jumped.

"I've heard enough," she said. "Bullpucky. That's a term we use up here." I think I was falling in love with Judge Anderson. Karen was going to have to watch herself. "I won't permit these kinds of delaying tactics. I'll give you three days to produce the financial information." She banged her gavel again and started to rise from the bench.

I leaped up. "Sanctions, your honor?"

She looked towards me but didn't pause in her ascendance. "I'm not going to impose sanctions at this time." Love's labor lost.

She gave the young lawyer another dirty look. She pointed her gavel at him as she stood behind the bench. "But don't push it."

I turned around to give Janet my best "see what a great lawyer I am" smile. But she was whispering something to Gino. His lips were drawn into a tight line as he listened. The corners of his mouth turned down. He leaned in closer and seemed to be intent on what Janet was saying to him.

For someone who had been bellyaching about how slow we were in getting Guyboy's financial information she seemed to have moved on quickly. I had no idea to where. Judging by the look on Bartoletti's face, I just hoped she wasn't talking about me.

It was one of those mornings at the beach that smelled strongly of seaweed caught by the on-shore breeze. The temperature was in the mid-60s and the clouds were shoving each other around like children on a playground.

It made me think of my old bachelor apartment on the Speedway in Venice Beach where I lived after I got divorced from my first wife. BK, before Karen. Mellow days of sun, sex and booze. When I used to get up with the sun and go to bed about the same time. I could still abuse my substance then. The good old days? It just seemed tiring now. Maybe I was getting old.

My receptionist, Pamela, and I were chatting at her desk in the living room we use as a lobby. I was trying my best not to go to work. Okay, I must admit I'm not the soul of industry. So there. It's out. I feel better.

She and I were discussing the latest problem with her boyfriend. Ah, to be young again. I had just raised a Diet Coke to my lips when the front door opened. A UPS man in brown looked over the top of a dolly that was piled high with legal file boxes. He gave us a friendly grin.

"I have a delivery for –- he looked at his clipboard –- the Law Offices of James Emerson Harris."

"That's us," I said, lowering the plastic bottle.

"Where do you want them?" He nodded at the stack of boxes.

I walked across to Karen's office and opened the door. "Put them in here," I said. Karen didn't object. Maybe because she was still at home with Bruno, sleeping in.

"Right," he said.

Wrong. I didn't ask him how many boxes he had. It took him almost 20 minutes. Half a truckload as it turned out. Now I know what Brown can do for me. I was in it up to my nose.

Campion & Gilbert had apparently changed tactics on us. They weren't holding out anymore. They were flooding us with everything they could get their hands on. Swift work for just one week. John Campion is an amazing guy when he puts his mind to it.

Looking at the boxes in Karen's office, I suspected she might not be pleased. They rose halfway to the ceiling around all four walls. Including the window. It made the room a tad dark. But gosh, we left her a six-foot path all the way to her desk.

I walked back across the lobby to Clyde's office and knocked on his open door. I poked my head in. He was immersed in making notes on a deposition he was reviewing. Clyde has great concentration when he's in the middle of something. That's why he can leave his door open. He looked up. I gave him my old 100 kilowatt smile. "Hi."

He knows me too well. Actually, it seems like everyone knows me too well these days. "Hi, yourself. How am I getting screwed this time?"

I tsked, tsked at him and motioned with my index finger for him to follow me. He got up reluctantly.

He took one look in Karen's office. "Oh, shit," he said. Clyde's losing his eloquence. He needs to work with me more.

"Do you think you can finish indexing these before Karen gets here?" My face was all innocence. So I'm an optimist.

"Is she on vacation?" He paused. "For maybe a month?" What happened to Clyde's "can do" spirit? Well, his hands weren't going to be the devil's tool for a while.

"Give me a list of the files in each box. A brief summary of each file would be useful. Chop, chop." I smiled and clapped him on the shoulder. He didn't reciprocate.

Hasn't he heard, if you were supposed to like it, they

wouldn't call it work.

Chapter 26

The sun was up and there was a cool on-shore breeze. White horses danced their jig on the top of choppy little waves. The breeze flecked at us with tiny pieces of foam.

It was pretty deserted at the beach except for a few early morning runners. Karen stopped as we reached the water and took my hand. She closed her eyes and tipped her face up to the sunshine. The breeze ruffled her short hair. Her face lights up when she smiles. God, I think she's beautiful. Bruno looked up at us and barked. He agrees with me.

We come down to the beach to run him. Running Bruno is a euphemism. But I've never heard of anyone waddling their dog. Bruno likes being out. He particularly likes the beach and we come down here pretty regularly.

Whenever we come down to the beach, Bruno always starts by barking furiously at the surf and chasing it away. Then he skitters back to us when it turns on him. Sometimes he's not fast enough. He shakes himself like crazy then and gets us all wet too. If we're not fast enough.

He's one funny dog. At four years old —- 28 in dog years -- you'd think he'd have learned something. Okay, so I didn't by the time I was 28, but Bruno's smarter. Anyway, he chases in and out maybe ten times before he concludes that the surf has had enough. Then he's ready to romp. .

Bruno's not too crazy about being run on his leash, even though we've got one of those things that go in and out on a spring. But we have to. Our police are ever diligent. They may not be adept at solving a shooting but there are no rampaging dogs in our town. And there are no dog parks. Poor Bruno. He bears up well.

At least Karen's speaking to me again. It's a step in the right direction.

She'd been less than pleased when she'd arrived with Bruno the morning of the delivery of all the boxes from John Campion. I had explained to her the boxes were part of my plan to bullet proof her office. It was for her own protection. I'm pretty sure, based on what she said, she didn't believe me.

I then pointed out that I was the lawyer and the boxes couldn't go in my office. That actually had been her second suggestion about where to put the boxes. The first was impractical. They wouldn't fit. Anyway, I put my foot down. You have to be masterful with these women. I can safely say she understood me perfectly.

It had taken Clyde a full month to get me a list of all the files that came from Guy Mason. We had been shipping the boxes to the accountant as fast we cataloged them. We were going to send off the last of them today.

I'd been sending copies of the list of contents of each box to Janet Mason as they were shipped. I wanted her to see what an industrious fellow she had hired. I also wanted to soften her up so I could ask her for more money. I'm devious, what can I say?

The best thing was, Karen was about to get her office back. I was hoping that my sex life would improve. Exist might be more accurate. My hand was getting tired of being my hand.

Even Bruno was annoyed with me. He wouldn't come sit in my lap. I even offered to let him look through the binoculars. I'd explained to him how inconvenient it would be for him -- not for me -- if we had all those boxes in my office. He didn't seem convinced.

The day after we shipped off the last box, Janet Mason called. Speaking to her is not the highlight of my day. I picked up the phone warily.

"Good morning," I said, mustering all the cheerfulness I could capture.

"Where are the files on Franklin Farms?"

She had me there. "They aren't in the boxes?"

"You idiot. Those are the critical files."

That was news to me. I seemed to recall she'd said that Franklin Farms was worthless. "Why?" I asked.

"Never mind," she snapped. "Here's what I need from you. I want to know every step you take to get those records. And I want particularly to know when you can expect to have them. Call me every two days. Do you think you can do that?" Her tone implied less than complete confidence.

"Sure."

"Are you going to schedule Guy's deposition?"

"As soon as Tony Thompson has an analysis of the financial records. Probably in about two weeks."

"Then set the deposition now. I want a copy of the papers with the time and place."

That was weird. Beyond just pushy. Janet was reaching for new heights here. Normally my clients don't do the scheduling for me. And why did she want it in writing? I could call and let her know the time and place if she cared to attend.

This was one strange lady. And I use the term loosely. Both terms.

Chapter 27

Karen rolled over and snuggled up against me. My first thought was it was my reward for sleeping on the wet spot last night. I was wrong.

"I'm going to miss you while I'm away." She kissed me above my right temple and gave me a squeeze.

I'd forgotten she was going down to L.A. to attend a NALA seminar and spend a couple of days with my mother. NALA is the law office administrator's organization. I think they were going to have a scintillating program on how to collect old accounts receivable or some such. Thank God, Karen likes all that stuff. The office would collapse without her. It may collapse anyway but it won't be her fault.

I turned over towards her and grazed her small, pink nipple with my fingernail. It stood up and said hello. She slapped at my hand and bolted out of bed.

"No time. I'm late."

"I'll miss you too," I said to her retreating back. "Give my love to mother."

I think my mother loves Karen more than she loves me. But then, I'm worried Karen loves Bruno more than me. I'm not paranoid. Hell, I love Bruno more than I love me. ."

The sun was shining. I said goodbye to Bruno. "I won't be long. Do you want me to bring you anything?" Bruno didn't respond so I figured he was full.

I had decided to walk to breakfast. Since Karen had taken the Jaguar it wasn't all that tough a decision. As I reached the corner of 4th and Main a gray Mercedes pulled up beside me. The back door swung open and there was my old friend Gino Bartoletti.

He raised his hand and drew two fingers towards himself. "Get in." He slid over.

The fireplug was driving.

"Thanks for the lift. I was just going another block to the Lilly Pad." I said it hopefully.

He turned to look at me. He has hard dark eyes.

"Or not," I said.

He grunted and turned to face forward. "Down by the coast. Drive." He made a gesture with the back of his hand towards the fireplug.

We drove in silence for a few minutes. I hoped I hadn't done anything to offend him. I'm sensitive to other people's feelings.

"I'm interested in the Franklin Farms project." He didn't turn to look at me.

"If it's about the entitlements, I didn't mean to cause you a problem." I may have said that a little quickly. But I wanted him to know we were still doing business together.

"Shut up."

"Sure."

"You're trying to get the financial records on Franklin Farms."

How did he know that?

"I don't want my name associated with that project," he said. "I wouldn't like that." I didn't know his name was associated with that project.

"Why?" Damn. I knew I shouldn't have asked that question the moment it popped out of my mouth.

He turned to look at me with those hard eyes. He wasn't smiling. I wasn't either.

I held up my hand with my palm up towards him and waved it from side to side. "Never mind," I said. I really meant it.

He turned back to face front and nodded but his jaw looked like granite. You'd be surprised how silent the inside of a Mercedes can become.

"Pull over," he said to the fireplug. He leaned across me and pushed opened the door. "Get out."

We had pulled up in front of McClintock's in Shell Beach. I got out and the Mercedes pulled smoothly away. Leaving me 20 miles from where I wanted to be. And grateful. I called a cab from the gas station across the road.

Bruno and I had had a long day at the office. I kept reflecting on my ride with Mr. Bartoletti. He didn't care that I was challenging the entitlements. He didn't want his name to be involved. What was that all about? I had no idea.

Bruno and I were baching it. "Come on Bruno," I said. "I'm cooking. Steaks tonight." Bruno's face lit up. I mean he really looked eager. He didn't remember we had to walk. Threess whole blocks. Uphill.

It gets dark early in winter. San Buenasera doesn't have sidewalks or streetlights. The town fathers contend they want to convey a rural feeling. I think they're just stealing the money. I envy them.

We made it home in five minutes. The house was dark. We walked up to the front door. I took out my key. Bruno went nuts. It was very unBruno like. He was snarling and running at the front door and then back again.

"What is it, boy? I laughed. I leaned down to scratch him behind his ear. "Is Timmy in the well?" Sometimes I'm not as swift as I think I am.

I opened the front door and walked in. As I reached for the light switch a large hard fist clobbered me on the side of the face. I went directly to the floor. I did not pass go. Bruno went under the couch. Smart dog. I wished I could join him. A big dark shape loomed over me.

"Mr. Bartoletti don't think you understood him too good. He thinks you got a smart mouth. I explain it to you." He grunted as he kicked me in the ribs. It hurt.

"I don't explain things so nice next time." Who was I to quibble? "You hear me." He kicked me again. I was not eager to make him work so hard.

I had my hands wrapped around my head and I was curled up in a ball to try to protect the family jewels. I was also nodding frantically. It occurred to me we were in the dark.

"Yes. Yes," I said. It came out louder than I had intended. "I understand. Don't kick me again. Please."

He was laughing as he left. I definitely wasn't. I lay still for a couple of minutes listening to the ringing in my ears. Bruno crawled over and started licking my face.

"Good dog." I reached up to pet him. The movement sent a sharp jolt of pain up my side. I carefully felt my ribs. I didn't think anything was broken. Then I felt my face. No blood. That was good. I sat up tentatively.

I groaned and lay back down. My head was spinning. I stayed put for ten minutes or so. Then I grabbed on to the arm of the couch and made it to my knees.

The light switch was a victory. I got into the bathroom with the assistance of a couple of walls. I shouldn't have looked into the mirror. I touched the side of my face. "Ouch."

A purple bruise was beginning to show. I was going to have a shiner in the morning. I got out a wash cloth and soaked it in hot water. It felt good as I dabbed it at a spot of blood at the corner of my mouth.

I found a hand towel, took it into the kitchen and wrapped up some ice and put it on my face. Bruno sat watching me. He barked. I'm sure he was concerned for my well-being. I moved my head too quickly as I looked down.

This was not good. What had I gotten myself into? Gino Bartoletti meant business and I didn't want to be on the other end. Things had gotten way serious when I hadn't been looking.

The only people who could have told him about the Franklin Farms records were Guy Mason or Janet. Excluding, of course, someone in the Campion firm or my office. Did it relate to Janet's lately expressed interest in the Franklin Farms records? Why should any of them tell him? And why should he care? At least enough to get him this angry.

Maybe it related to the federal raid at the union pension fund. Or maybe not. I certainly had a lot of questions along with a very sore face. I'd better figure out how to get some answers. I wanted to stay out of Mr. Bartoletti's way. The only good thing I could think of was Karen hadn't been here.

Bruno barked, interrupting my train of thought.

"Don't worry, boy, I'll be okay." I said it absently. I was trying to concentrate on thinking this through.

He barked again and I looked down at him. He was wagging his tail eagerly. He barked a third time. When you've lived with Bruno for a while you get to understand him. He has different barks for different occasions and he's quite expressive. He lifted an eyebrow at me.

Apparently neither time, nor tide, nor Bruno's dinner waits for any man.

Chapter 28

"That's some shiner. What happened?" Clyde said. He pulled out my client chair and sat down.

Apparently, sneaking into the office early in the morning hadn't been entirely successful. But Bruno and I needed to get some papers. That's where Clyde found us. I had called in sick the last couple of days. I was nursing my bruised ribs and icing my face. The swelling was pretty much gone but my shiner had bloomed into shades of purple and green. I was a gardener's delight.

"I ran into a fireplug."

"How'd you manage that?"

"Don't ask." For once, I was serious. He shouldn't know. If I told him, he might be the next one getting hurt.

Clyde pointed to my eye. "Big fireplug, huh?"

I didn't respond to his question. Frankly, I didn't know what to say. So I shrugged.

He gave me the raised eyebrow. "When's Karen coming back?"

"Tomorrow."

"She's going to go crazy."

"Yeah, I guess."

Karen had been calling every evening to talk to me and Bruno, but I hadn't told her about my visit with the fireplug. Neither had Bruno. We didn't want to worry her and besides I didn't want her rushing back up to San Buenasera until I figured something out.

I couldn't make heads or tails of what was going on. And I was concerned for Karen too. Maybe more than for me. I don't know what would have happened if she'd been with me. I didn't care to think about it.

I cut to the chase with Clyde. "I think we should lay off trying to get the financial information on Franklin Farms."

I could see the pieces of the puzzle come together in his eyes, but he just said, "You're a little late, boss. I got those files and shipped them over to Tony Thomson." Clyde crossed his legs and changed position. He gave me his killer smile.

Oh, great. First we can't get anything. Now John Campion is just dying to co-operate. Speaking of dying, I hope he isn't trying to get me killed? Could he have told Bartoletti? Just kidding. Maybe.

"When did it come in?"

"Yesterday. Arrived by UPS in the morning delivery. I asked Tony to take a quick look at it. I thought you'd want to get back to Janet Mason. Besides, the deposition of Guy Mason is set for next week unless the judge postpones it. Mason's law firm's filed another motion." Clyde gave his "why me" expression. I ignored it. Hard work is good for him.

I'd forgotten about the deposition. I wished them lots of luck with Judge Anderson.

"You haven't told Janet we got the files, have you?" My voice may have been a wee bit tense. To tell you the truth, I was scared. I didn't know who was doing what to whom or what could inspire another encounter with Mr. Bartoletti or his myrmidon. The only thing I was clear on was such an encounter was something I very much wanted to avoid.

Clyde gave me a strange look. "Nope. I leave that important kind of stuff to you." Clyde didn't like Janet Mason either.

"We'd better see what Tony found out, I guess." I reached for the phone without much enthusiasm. I wasn't anxious to dig deeper into Franklin Farms. But it was better than sticking my head in the sand. Or someplace riskier.

Tony Thompson looks like an accountant. He's tall and a little stooped. His brown hair is thinning. He's got an aquiline nose upon which his thick glasses perch precariously. He carries an old brown leather briefcase. I always picture him in a green eye-shade and plastic cuffs. But he's good. Even if he is in San Buenasera.

Tony had walked over to visit with us. He held out his hand. I took it. Bruno waddled over to say hello. Tony bent down at the knees to tug on his ear.

"Hey, Bruno," Tony said, and gave Bruno's nose a brisk rub. Bruno's a neighborhood favorite. I know for a fact he's thinking of running for mayor. "You look a lot better than your boss. He looks like hell." Tony looked up at me and nodded at my face. "That must hurt."

"Yeah, it does," I said. I wasn't kidding. My eye was throbbing. Clyde dragged in another chair.

He shook hands with Clyde.

"I was wondering . . ." I started. Tony held up his hand.

"Hold on a minute." Tony's a very organized guy. I guess that's good for an accountant. He lifted his briefcase onto the chair and opened it. He started sorting out his notes.

"You want some coffee or a Diet Coke?" I asked.

He shook his head without looking up. He sat down and tapped his stack of pages into order, first one way, then the other, and placed them on my desk, precisely in front of him. Then Tony looked up at me with an expectant expression. "Anytime."

I obliged. "What did you find out about Franklin Farms?"

"Your client was right. It's worthless. At least to Guy Mason. I've never seen such convoluted financing. The property secures three separate trust deeds. All the lenders are offshore companies."

"Who are they?"

"I have the names off the trust deeds, but I don't think it's going to help. I never heard of any of them. I tried to track them down on the Internet. Found absolutely nothing about them."

"That's unusual," I said.

"You bet. There's usually lots of information on lending institutions. And these loans add up to more than the purchase price. I checked the tax records. They total about $25 million."

"Wow. You mean the land cost that much?"

"Yeah, it did. $22,000,000. At least when you add in all the costs of plans and everything."

"Does that make any sense?

"You mean the loans?"

"No." I was curious. I might want to go into the development business myself one day. "I mean a project like that."

Tony gave me a funny look. I guess he didn't think I had the developer stuff. "Jimmy, a project like Franklin Farms will cost about a half billion dollars to build. It takes about $100 million dollars in equity. I roughed out the numbers because I wanted to see what kind of financing commitments were required."

I have to say I was impressed.

"Can Guy Mason make money with costs like that?" I asked.

"You mean if he can get it built?"

I nodded. I can dream.

"If he builds 800 homes. Only about $600 million. Maybe more."

I whistled. "That's a lot of money." I'm a genius at stating the obvious.

"It's a huge project. That's the problem. It's too large. It's way out of Guy Mason's league. That's what makes the financing so strange."

"Why?"

"Well, to start with, where is Mason going to get $75 million dollars more? And it doesn't make any sense, at least for a lender. They never put up the first money. There isn't any equity cushion under them to protect the loans. I don't know why a lender would do that. And they must be sure that the $75 million will come from somewhere. Otherwise, they'll be left high and dry. But there's no indication they could know."

"Could Guy Mason be fronting for someone?" Clyde asked. Clyde's a smart boy. I think I mentioned that.

"Maybe. It's the only possibility I can think of," Tony said. "Until the entitlements are cleared and the land can be developed, there's no equity value in it. Only more cost. And enormous risk."

"Any idea why he might be doing that?" I said.

"Well, I haven't finished reviewing all those other files you sent over, but from what I've seen, Guy Mason is in financial trouble. All kinds of lawsuits and foreclosures. I'd say he looks to be flat broke other than for some term life insurance he's got. He can't borrow against that. No equity value. This might be the only way he could do a deal."

"So someone else might own the project and Mason might be getting some kind of profit participation for fronting it?" Clyde said.

Someone like Gino Bartoletti came to my mind.

"Could be," Tony said. "I had another real estate deal a while ago where some guy who had been in prison for fraud wanted to do a deal but figured the county wouldn't be too hot on dealing with an ex-con. So he got this young fellow to put the land in his name so the project could go forward. Promised him 20% of the profits. Good deal for the young fellow. Made a lot of money. It could be the same thing here."

Something I really didn't want to know.

Chapter 29

"Oh, my gosh. What happened? Why didn't you tell me? What . . ."

Karen's back. It was about 10:00 in the morning and she'd come straight to the office. She ran over to me and gave me a hug. "Poor baby." She stepped back a little lightly touched the edge of my eye with her finger.

I winced and pulled my head back. "Ouch."

"How did this happen?" Her voice was firmer now.

"Let's talk about it later when I can tell you everything." I wasn't happy about the thought of this conversation. I was trying to put it off as long as possible. "Maybe we'll go home for lunch."

I didn't want to tell her about it. But, it could be more dangerous for her unless she knew what was going on. That felt really shitty to admit to myself. I had gotten us into a rotten situation. And these weren't petty drug dealers. This could be big time bad stuff.

Her mouth firmed up and she looked like she was going to object. Then she seemed to catch herself and reluctantly agreed. "Lunch!"

I took a bite of my turkey and Swiss on rye. It was totally appropriate. I was the turkey with the black eye.

We were at our kitchen table. It was cloudy so we had the light on. I felt a little like I was in an interrogation.

Karen was nibbling at a tuna sandwich. She's naturally the daintiest eater you can imagine. I don't know why. There's not an ounce of fat on her.

"Okay," she said, "I want to know what happened." It wasn't a question. It was a direction. Karen's tough.

I took a swig of Diet Coke and cleared my throat. Truth be told, I wanted a drink. I wanted a drink more than I'd wanted one in three years. Karen would kill me. Besides, I knew I had to keep my wits about me or Gino Bartoletti might kill me. Whatever wits I could muster.

"It was Gino Bartoletti. Actually his goon. Mr. Bartoletti wanted to make a point. He doesn't want his name associated with Franklin Farms."

Her eyes hardened. "What does he have to do with Franklin Farms?"

"I don't know. Maybe he provided the financing."

"So what?"

"I have no idea. The Feds just raided the pension fund he controls. That could have something to do it. But who knows. The financing wasn't in the name of the pension fund. And Mr. Bartoletti wasn't very forthcoming."

She stayed quiet for a moment. I could see her thinking it through. Picturing what happened.

"Jimmy, I don't like this. I'm scared. Someone came into our house and beat you up." Smart girl. "You've got to get out of these cases. It isn't worth it."

I leaned back in my chair and sighed. "I know. But it's such good money. I thought we were going to finally get out of debt and maybe have a little money to put aside."

She put her hand on mine and squeezed. "We'll be okay. I don't want you to get hurt."

I didn't either. And God forbid anything should happen to her.

"You're right. I'll tell Janet Mason today. I'm being dumb." She gave me an impish smile and nodded. I wanted to hug her. In fact that's exactly what I did.

We've been together eight years now and I still love to hug her. There's something about the way she fits. Maybe it's because we're not married. But I don't think so.

"I'm so glad you're back. I missed you," I said, my voice muffled by her red hair.

"I missed you, too, you old, beat up lawyer. I love you."

Can you believe it? There was a tear in my eye. Must be allergies.

"You look like shit," Janet Mason said. It was becoming a refrain. She was sitting out by her pool in a skimpy bikini. The edge of one nipple poked up out of its cup. I don't think Janet Mason cared. It would have been thought provoking at some other time.

"What happened?" she said. Her tone didn't exactly drip with interest. But finally, here was a question I wanted to answer.

"Your friend Gino Bartoletti had me beat up." Her hand went to her mouth. It reminded me of a scene in the "Big Sleep". I'm just a cynical guy, I guess.

"Oh, I'm so sorry."

"Were you the one who told him I was subpoenaing the Franklin Farms documents from your husband?"

She considered that. "I may have," she said slowly. "I didn't think it would mean anything." She shifted her position on the chaise lounge.

"It did. I don't appreciate being beat up, Janet. I'm withdrawing from all your matters. As of now."

She seemed surprised. Maybe even distressed. This was not the Janet Mason I knew. She swung herself into a sitting position and put her hand on my arm. She leaned towards me. Her breast came all of the way out of its cup. She didn't notice. At least I don't think she did. I didn't notice. It was conically shaped with a prominent brown nipple set at an upward angle. I swear, it was only a glance.

"Please, Jimmy." Since when did she call me Jimmy? "I need you." She moved towards me. Her breast pressed into my arm. I felt a heat flash. "You're the only lawyer I've ever trusted." That was news to me, but it felt good. The breast, I mean.

Then I remembered the agenda. "Janet, that's bullshit." I moved my arm away from her. "You've been nothing but critical and condescending since we started working together. I thought you'd be happy."

A tear rolled down her cheek. Then another. "I know I've been a bitch." She put her hand on my arm again. "I've been under so much pressure. Please forgive me. I really like you." I have never heard the work "like" said with so many overtones. But I was strong. Also, my eye was throbbing.

"Look, Janet, I'll forgive you, I just don't want anything to do with your legal matters." However, I didn't move my arm away.

"Let me talk to Gino. He's really not like that. I'll make him apologize. It won't happen again. I promise you. He just made a mistake."

"That was a hell of a mistake."

"I know. He just doesn't realize how important you are to me. Will you let me talk to him? Just give me a chance before you do anything. Please. And I promise, I'll make it up to you. I will." I had no idea what she meant, but the nipple on her breast was standing at attention. It was tempting, but I resisted the impulse to salute. Gino had already given me an eyeful.

"Look, I can't file withdrawal papers until tomorrow. I don't think there's anything you can do that will make me change my mind."

"Jimmy, just don't do anything until I get back to you, okay?" She gave me her television smile. Then she looked down. "Oh, my goodness," she said, tucking her breast back into its cup. But she said it with a smile.

"Okay." I said it reluctantly. I knew I was making a mistake. I'm a sucker for a beautiful woman. Maybe Janet really did need me. Or I'm just stupid.

Chapter 30

"It's Dom Perignon," I said to Karen, pointing at the box. There was a sense of wonder in my voice. I don't think I'd ever seen a whole case of it.

We were gathered around a rough wooden box that had been in the middle of my desk when I arrived the next morning. It had a big yellow bow on top. The name and crest of the champagne house were burned into the ends. The box had come with a letter from Janet Mason. I had pried the lid off the box and a musty smell had filled the room.

I'm a great lawyer, but people aren't always as insightful as they might be. Few of my clients send me gifts. Even the ones who pay their bills.

I dug out one of the tightly corked bottles and studied the label. "2004," I said, tapping my lips sagely with the tip of a finger. "Umm. Good year." I don't know anything about wine. I don't drink anymore. And when I had, I drank beer. Karen knew that.

She punched me in the shoulder and gave me one of her looks. "Don't be a smart-ass."

"A whole case," I said. "This stuff costs a fortune," That much I knew. "It came with this letter from Janet Mason." I passed it over to her.

She took the letter out of the envelope and quickly read through it.

"There's a check in there too," I said pointing at the envelope.

She gasped appropriately at the $20,000 check. She made a sharp little movement with her head. "Do you trust her? Janet Mason?"

I avoided the question. "Well, she said in the letter that Gino was really sorry. Just an awful misunderstanding. The champagne is from him. It was a nice gesture, don't you think?"

I'm an optimist. That's someone who goes around saying this is the best of all possible worlds. A pessimist is someone who agrees with him.

"I don't know. How can you be so sure Gino Bartoletti actually said it was a mistake?"

"I can't exactly call him and ask, you know." I may have been a little sharp. After all, I don't have Gino's home telephone number. Given that he had sicced his goon on me, for what I didn't know, having his telephone number could be downright bad news. My black eye throbbed in sympathy. "Why would she lie?" I asked.

"I don't know. Maybe to keep you involved in the lawsuits." The golden specks in her eyes danced prominently in the sunlight when she looked directly at me.

"She could get another lawyer. Easy." I made a sweeping gesture with my hand.

"Sure, but that would take time. She could be concerned about delay for some reason." Karen was stretching.

"I don't see it."

"Are you going to stay in the cases?" Her voice was anxious.

I hadn't asked for the $20,000. It was a lot of money. People don't throw that around. It made me wonder. But people don't turn it away that easily either. I sure don't.

Karen put her hand on my arm and looked deeply into my eyes. I opened them widely. I tried hard to look innocent. That's not so easy for me. Particularly with her.

Things hadn't been going all that well in my practice since we moved up to San Buenasera. We weren't behind in our house payments anymore, thank goodness. We paid the mortgage up with part of Janet's original retainer. But I was worried about how we were going to make next month's payment.

And we hadn't paid our property taxes in three years. After five years they sell your house out from under you. I also had a stack of past due bills for the law firm. I was letting them mellow in my desk drawer. Janet was the biggest client I'd had in a long time.

"I admit it's tempting. And with Guy Mason's deposition coming up next week, I'm not so sure the court will let us out now anyway. Janet did apologize again for giving us a hard time." I pointed at the letter Karen was still holding. "She's had a lot of stress." I'm great at rationalizing.

That's when Bruno had his attack of flatulence. To his credit it was a dainty fart. Dainty but powerful.

"Whew." I waived my hand in front of my face.

"Bruno!" Karen said.

Bruno looked up from his spot on the couch where he was engaged in innocently licking his balls. He has very expressive eyes. "What?" they said. "It was the big blond guy standing next to you who gave me the broccoli last night."

I thought that was unfair. Bruno likes broccoli more than I do. And I like to share. But I couldn't stand the smell, so I went over to the window.

As I was raising the sash, I thought I caught a glimpse of
Clarence, the undertaker. He's still pissed with me. We filed
a motion for contempt last week when he didn't pay his child
support. I needed Clarence like a hole in the head right now.
I had a lot bigger problems. So I ignored him. I turned back
to Karen, still waving my hand in front of my face. I made
my way over to my desk and sat down.

"I'm not going to say don't do it," Karen said reluctantly.
"Just think about it before you decide." There was a plea in
her voice. "I know we need the money. But I don't like it and
I don't trust Janet Mason. There's something spooky about
that woman."

I wasn't happy about the thought of getting beat up again.
Or putting Karen in danger. She seemed small and
vulnerable just then.

I made a decision. This was tough. I let out a sigh.
"Karen, I need to be serious." Damn, I hate that. I motioned
for her to sit down. I sat down myself. This wasn't like me. I
like to keep things light.

She nodded and sat down. She was looking at me intently.
I think I surprised her. And maybe I scared her a bit.

"I'm frightened to death of Gino Bartoletti," I said. "He's a
big time hood and I've never dealt with anyone like him
before. I'm not only frightened for me. I'm frightened for
you too. I wouldn't want to put you in danger for the world."

A tear ran down her cheek.

"And I don't know how good an actress Janet Mason is. You asked me whether I trust her. I want to. We really need this money. If Janet has gotten Gino Bartoletti off my back, it's a shame to pass it up."

"But I feel like it could be dangerous," she said.

"I know. But maybe there's a way we can do this. If I just take Guyboy's deposition next week, I think the court will let me out. I won't be holding Janet up then. She might even agree. I think we'll be okay for a week. Can you go along with that?"

Karen was quiet. The silence hung in the air between us. Her face was a blank.

"Just a week more?" she said.

"I promise you we'll get out then."

She finally nodded. "I think we can do that. I hope so."

I went around the desk and took her into my arms. She was shaking. I stroked her hair. "It'll be okay, baby," I said. I hoped I was doing the right thing.

But I found out a week can be a very long time. God was exhausted after six days.

Chapter 31

I grew up poor. Not skid row poor. Just ordinary poor. Mom raised me and my brother by working 12 hours a day in a little grocery store. My father died in a car crash when I was eight. He was drunk.

My brother got the brains. He's a college professor in Midland, Texas. I got the good looks and charm. We were never close.

I wasn't a great student, but you know how California is. I went to a community college where I was better with the girls than with my books. That was okay by me. I got laid a lot. I made it into Cal State Long Beach by the skin of my teeth, which is the way I got out. A political science major. The definition of politics? "Poly", Latin meaning many. "Tics", English meaning blood-sucking vermin. It appealed to me.

Oh, and I got married in my last year in college. She was a looker. Carrie Moss. It didn't last. Four years, over and out. I wasn't communicative enough. Ms. Moss hated my sense of humor. And I left the toilet seat up.

I think she may have become perturbed when she got up in the middle of the night to use the bathroom. It was quiet for a moment or two. Then I heard a splash.

I didn't even know she knew some of those words. It may not have been helpful that I was giggling uncontrollably when she returned to our soon to be ex-conjugal bed. We all make mistakes.

After graduating I found myself well qualified to do various janitorial tasks. Actually, I worked on a lot of construction jobs. I hated it. It was really hard work.

That was my motivation for going to night school to study law. Western States School of Law. I think it's accredited now. Law was as close to politics as I could get.

After passing the bar, I finally landed a job with the public defender's office. I'm proud of the fact I passed the bar the very first time I really applied myself. The third time I took it if I recall correctly. Those five years with the public defender led me to being the great lawyer I am today.

Which all goes to say I didn't want to be poor again, which is why I tucked away that $20,000 check from Janet Mason in our bank account. And why Tony Thompson, Clyde and I were sitting around the coffee table in my office at nine o'clock on a Monday night going through Guy Mason's financial records preparing for his deposition. I had all the lights on and it still seemed dim to me. The darkness pushing up against the windows closes you in.

Bruno had left with Karen, otherwise the boxes of cold pizza lying around on the floor would have been empty. Bruno likes to play with girls more than boys. Smart dog.

We had been at it for several hours and we were getting a tad grumpy. I tossed another report back on the coffee table, stood up and rubbed the nine o'clock shadow on my face. I twisted my arms back and forth behind my back, then over my head and groaned.

"Damn, I'm tired," I said. I reached down and picked up a cold slice of pepperoni and took a bite. I chewed daintily. I like cold pizza. Especially for breakfast.

"It's your own fault, boss," Clyde said. "You could've lost the motion to delay the deposition."

"Why didn't I think of that," I said between swallows. "It's just that I like to see Judge Anderson torturing those big city lawyers. I lost my head."

Tony wasn't finding this amusing. "Come on, Jimmy. Sit down and let's get this over with." He made a sharp motion with his hand. "The deposition is Wednesday and we've still got stuff left to go over." He took off his glasses and rubbed at his eyes.

The pizza made me thirsty. I walked through the

reception area to the little refrigerator in Karen's office and got a Diet Coke. "You guys want anything?" I called out. The response wasn't overwhelming. I popped open the can with one hand, took a swig and wandered back into the room.

"Okay, let's get going." I stifled a yawn and plopped down on the sofa next to Clyde, Diet Coke in one hand, pizza in the other. Fully armed. I put my feet up on the coffee table and laid my head against the back of the couch and yawned.

Tony brandished a few pages of paper. "It came out like I guessed, more or less. Mason may be able to hold onto his apartment project in San Diego. Maybe. He's playing chicken with the bank. His two projects in Costa Mesa are in deep trouble."

Clyde got to his feet and started wandering around the room. "Sorry, need to stretch my legs," he said.

Tony looked up and then glanced at his papers again. "His partners are suing him for fraudulently diverting funds. They've got forensic accountants crawling all over him. I think he's going to get creamed. It's the kind of thing that could bring him down."

"How does he live so high?" I asked from my semi-supine position. I mean, maybe I could learn something. I had an uncle once whose business went bankrupt. He came to see me so I could explain to him how he could be bankrupt when he had money coming into the business every day. I bet he still had checks in his checkbook too.

"Mason has enough things going that he can juggle everything and pull money from here and there to pay whoever has to be paid. Keeps everybody a little happy. At least not unhappy enough to cut him off. No one wants to kill the goose that lays the golden egg unless it stops laying."

I raised my head. "Any bank accounts we can grab?"

"Overdrawn."

"He still has the big house."

"Oh, sure. And a big mortgage. I doubt there's any equity. Besides his bank has a second."

"You make it sound like he's living off fumes."

"I've seen it before. Someone like Guy Mason can go on a long time. Then he just cracks. I think he's close."

Clyde had resumed his seat and was making notes. He looked up. "How close? We want to get a piece of him before he tanks."

"That's hard to say. But the situation I see with Franklin Farms makes me think he's desperate."

"Have you found out anything more about the financing or those off-shore companies?" I asked.

"Nope. Nothing I can find out. You'd have to be the Feds

to sort it out. Tax haven secrecy. Shell companies. Cross ownership. But it looks fishy."

That gave me a problem. Did I want to touch that financing? I wasn't sure it made any difference to Janet. Not that I cared much. Getting beat up wasn't part of my job description.

The financing arrangement with whomever was whatever it was and if Mason got some money out of Franklin Farms we could glom onto it. If Gino Bartoletti was involved with the financing I wanted to stay as far away as I could. I didn't have any faith that Gino was really off my back. I was trying here to hump a camel through the eye of a needle and get the hell out.

I might be able to scare Mason without actually getting into the financing. It was something to think about. But then he'd already offered a great settlement that Janet had turned down cold. Maybe she thought he couldn't pay. Who knows?

"I guess we've gone as far as we can," I said. "Let's call it a night." I took my feet off the coffee table with a thump.

I struggled to a standing position. I turned to Clyde who was gathering his notes. "Why don't you put together some questions tomorrow we can use at the deposition. Then you and I can go over them in the afternoon. I want you to sit with me Wednesday morning."

I didn't need Clyde, of course. I knew what I was doing. I just wanted him to see the master in action and learn. Absolutely.

"Sure, boss," he said.

Tony also struggled to his feet.

"Tony, thanks for coming over. You did a great job." I held out my hand and he took it.

Tony looked me in the eyes. "Jimmy, I'm not sure there's anything here for Janet Mason," he said. "I think you need to tell her."

"I already tried, Tony. But I'll try again when we get the deposition finished." Just before I file my motion to be relieved. Just as soon as this deposition was over.

Tony and I walked out together. Clyde was closing up. It was a cool, moist night with a bit of a breeze. There was a full moon.

"Can I give you a lift?" I said.

"It's only a couple of blocks. I think I'll walk. We've been cooped up all day."

"Great. Thanks again." I waved to his back and turned towards the Jaguar.

There were three deep gouges in the paint where someone had scratched it with a key.

Chapter 32

I was singing "When the Saints Go Marchin' In" as I was shaving. I can't remember the words. I make them up as I go along. A lot like my law practice.

It was Wednesday. D Day. The day of Guy Mason's deposition. I was prepared and ready to go. I had it made.

Nothing but a few scratches on the car. And that was Clarence, I figured. I was going to have to do something about him when I was shunt of the Masons, Guy and Janet.

One depo, then I was out one way or another. And $20,000 richer. I was in fine voice.

I wiped the shaving cream off my face. I turned my face left and right to the mirror. I looked fine. Karen was wandering around the house in her short, black teddy and high rise black lace underwear. She looked fine too.

"Today's the day," I said to her.

She came over and gave me a hug. She looked up and

held me in those big eyes. "I'm proud of you. Go sic 'em, tiger."

I slid my hand under her teddy and fingered her nipple. "For luck," I said. I'm incorrigible. She likes me that way. She must. She just smiled up at me. I'm easily incorriged.

I figured I'd take the deposition, then pull Janet aside to discuss releasing me from the representation. I also wanted to talk to her about Tony Thompson's concerns, but that wasn't much of an issue since I didn't expect it to be my problem.

The deposition was scheduled to start at 10 o'clock in our conference room. Our conference room is really Clyde's office. It's also our library. The room has a long table and is lined with law books from floor to ceiling on three walls.

It's an idea I had to give the place some pizzazz. No one uses law books anymore. Everything's on computer. So law books are a dime a dozen. But they make a great stage prop, at least if you don't know we never use them. And they also cover the water stains on the walls.

Clyde had put away his things. God knows where. If you opened the closet door you might be crushed. The only thing on the conference table was Clyde's laptop. The place looked like a real law office conference room.

All the lights had been turned on to counter the gloom outside. It was one of those threatening days. No rain yet.

A table with coffee, Diet Cokes and sweet rolls had been set up in the corner. We do things right.

Our deposition reporter was putting together her little stenographic machine on its metal tripod. Margaret Simmons was our regular stenographer. She had a fresh roll of paper tape sitting on the corner of the table. She looked up as I came in.

"Hi, Maggie," I said. She'd carried us through some rough financial times, deferring invoices until I settled a case and the like. We were old friends.

Graham Southland arrived lugging a big black leather litigation case stamped in gold leaf with "C & G" on top. It looked like the brief case would bring him down. But he successfully made it into the room. The brief case made a thud when it hit the floor. I felt sorry for the floor.

Graham's the tall, thin, young lawyer taking all the abuse from Judge Anderson after John Campion made his one and only appearance. I guess this deposition didn't warrant an appearance by the great man. That was okay with me.

I held out my hand. "Hey, Graham. Make yourself at home. This is our little office." I made a sweeping gesture with my hand. He looked around with obvious distaste. It wasn't your average big city practice.

"A cup of coffee?" I motioned at the small table in the corner. He shook his head. I don't think he had the guts. No telling what disease he might pick up.

"This is Margaret Simmons, our reporter," I said.

He nodded towards her.

"Call me Maggie," she said. He looked a little startled. Apparently in L.A., stenographers were seen and not heard.

"You remember Clyde," I said.

"Sure." Graham and Clyde shook hands.

We settled in. Then we waited. 10:15 and Guy Mason hadn't shown. At 10:30 Janet Mason blew in.

"Oh, good. I'm not late." She looked great in her demure blue suit. The skirt was too short for modesty, but then modesty wasn't Janet's game. She had on a cream colored silk blouse that I bet cost more than my law office furniture. At least all of her was tucked in.

"We're still waiting for your husband," I said.

"He's never on time." Now there was a case of the pot and the kettle. "He'll be late for his own funeral."

Was that a joke? If so, she needed to work on her delivery. It sucked.

She turned to me. "James." I almost didn't respond. I didn't know she was speaking to me. I raised my head. "Can I speak to you for a second while we're waiting?"

"Of course. Let's go into my office." Janet and I rose. "Clyde, call us when Mr. Mason shows up."

I closed the door of my office behind us. "What can I do for you, Janet?"

"First, let me thank you for staying in the case. I'm sorry about what happened with Gino." She didn't mention the $20,000 check, which I thought was delicate. "He gets so impetuous."

That was a new word for it. I nodded. I didn't want to speak since I knew I didn't intend to stay in the case for very long. She switched gears. Her mouth turned down into a frown.

"A rather disturbing thing happened yesterday." She fidgeted, her hands moving uncertainly on the Gucci handbag she was holding. Her six carat diamond danced in the light.

"Oh?"

"Yes. Some men from the State showed up."

"Really. Did you ask to see identification?"

"They showed me some cards. I don't understand that kind of thing." She waved it away.

I grunted.

"Yes, they said they were from the State Bureau of Archeology."

Shit. I'd forgotten about the archeologists. I hope it didn't screw up any chance of a settlement. I bravely withheld any comment of my involvement.

"They said they needed to conduct a survey. They gave me this paper." She dug in her handbag and handed me an official looking order.

I started to read the paper. Without looking up I said, "Why didn't you call me?"

"I tried. They said you were out and they couldn't disturb you."

"True." I had been home preparing for the deposition. If I hadn't been napping. I try to concentrate my energy for these big legal battles.

I raised my head from my study of the order. "Let me look into this," I said, as I folded up the paper and laid it in the middle of my desk. I said it with authority.

I'm sure my tone implied I would take these guys to the cleaners. I had no idea what I was going to do. Probably nothing since I intended to be well out of this case by tonight.

"Maybe we should get back in there," I said. "I'm sure your husband will be here any second. By the way, after the deposition could you spare me a few moments?"

"Of course. What's it about?"

"Let's talk about it then. I don't want to distract us. This deposition's the most important thing right now."

She bought that. I held the door for her.

The atmosphere in the conference room was desultory. Everyone was bored. Clyde was sipping a Diet Coke. Graham Southland was doodling. No Guy Mason. It was 10:45.

I had left the door of the conference room open. Bruno poked his nose in. He was supposed to stay in Karen's office when we had a deposition, but Bruno's naturally inquisitive. Karen must have turned her back for a moment.

I hadn't noticed Bruno so he padded across the room and put his head in Maggie's lap. Bruno likes Maggie. In fact, Bruno likes all women. With the apparent exception of Janet Mason.

Maggie looked down. "Hello, Bruno honey," she said, giving him a scratch behind the ears. "How's my sweet dog?"

I thought Graham was going to have a kitten, which would have been interesting under the circumstances. Apparently dogs don't wander into his depositions. So I introduced them. He didn't shake hands. That's when Karen popped in to retrieve Bruno. It was 11:00. I glanced at my watch meaningfully.

Graham shifted uncomfortably. "I'm sure he'll be here soon. I tried to call him. I can't imagine what's holding him up."

Noon. "This is outrageous," I said. I stood up. "We're going into court for sanctions."

Maggie started to break down her stenographer's machine. Clyde leaned back and took it all in, a vacant smile on his lips.

"There's some good reason for my client's tardiness," Graham Southland said, laying both hands on the conference room table. His voice was firm, his manner sure. I admired the boy's poise.

Then he stood up and started packing his papers back in the big black briefcase. He turned to me and screwed on his courtroom face. "I'm going to find out what happened, he said. "We'll get back to you."

I wasn't about to hold my breath. But as it turned out, Graham was right. There was a very good reason.

Chapter 33

I was pretty pissed. Here it was Thursday afternoon. I still hadn't heard a word from Campion & Gilbert about why their client had stiffed us. It was a windy day. The clouds looked as if wispy lines had been brushed over a pale blue background.

Clyde had slapped together a motion for sanctions and an order to compel Guy Mason to submit to be deposed. The draft was on my desk. I just didn't have the energy to pick it up.

I was still in this damn case. And now I had no idea how long it was going to take to get me out. Karen, who usually takes things in stride, was down in the dumps. We had moped together all last night. Even Bruno was avoiding me.

I was brooding on all this with my feet up on my desk. I had pushed back with my hands behind my head. The ceiling in my office was flaking. I was going to have to get it painted one of these days.

I had almost reached the point where I wasn't going to wallow in self-pity any longer. Not quite, but almost. I was even eyeing Clyde's draft motion over the top of my moccasins. I have very well formed ankles. Everyone comments on them.

Then the phone rang. I came forward with a thud.

"James Emerson Harris."

"Mr. Harris, this is Chief Carsone." Whoopee. Just the person to lift my spirits. At least I could complain about Clarence, the undertaker.

"What can I do for you, Chief. Did you learn anything about who shot up my office?"

"Nope. You know a Guy Mason?"

He had my attention. I couldn't tell if he was asking a question or making a statement. Everyone in town knew I was representing Janet in her divorce. Word might have even reached our constabulary.

"I'm representing Mrs. Mason in her divorce. I've met Mr. Mason. I don't know him. Why?" I shifted the phone from one hand into the other and grabbed a pad to start making notes. Where the hell were all my pencils?

"When was the last time you saw him?"

"I don't know. Maybe a few weeks ago." I fumbled around in my top drawer. I was going to have to clean it out one of these days. When I wasn't so busy. I lifted a couple of rulers. There was one of the little yellow devils. I snatched it up. The tip was broken off. I pushed around in the drawer some more and found another one. Ever resourceful. Never pointless.

"You notice anything?"

"Like what, Chief?"

"You know. Like was he moody?" I dropped the pencil on my desk and ran my hand over my face. This guy was an idiot.

"I'm suing the man for divorce," I said. "Why wouldn't he be moody?"

"Don't know? Asking you."

"Why are you asking me?"

"Found your card in his car."

Ah. "That figures. He was supposed to appear at our offices for his deposition yesterday. He didn't show up."

"No, I suppose not."

What did that mean?

"Is there some reason he didn't show up, Chief. Did he have an accident?"

"Maybe. Can't say." I could almost see the smirk on his face. I wanted to reach down the phone line and grab him by the throat.

"Why not?"

"Don't comment on open cases." Our chief has been watching too much television. I picked up my pencil and broke it in two. I think its called sublimation.

I took another tack. "I'm just about to file a motion to compel Mr. Mason to appear. Should I delay filing?"

"Maybe."

Clyde poked his head into the office. I motioned him into the client chair and mouthed "Chief Carsone". I pointed at the receiver. Then I picked up the stub of my pencil and scratched "Guy Mason" on my pad and held it up in front of me. Clyde nodded. I hit the speakerphone button so we both could hear.

"Look, Chief," I said, "it would be helpful to the court to know when to schedule the deposition. I'd like to tell Judge Anderson your opinion. I'm sure she'd appreciate it." And maybe even vote for you when you run again in the next election. I hadn't lived in a small town for eight years and not know how it works. Clyde looked puzzled by all this but he catches up fast.

Carsone sounded a little more uncertain. "Maybe you should hold up on filing that motion," he said. Clyde spread his hands and brought his shoulders together. I gave him my "I wish I knew" look with my eyebrows and a shrug of the shoulder.

"Oh, I've got to file today," I said. I wasn't going to let Carsone off the hook. "We need to proceed. Our client is anxious." I crossed my legs and leaned back in my desk chair. I shut my mouth and waited. I counted to five.

"See, I don't think you have to rush like that," the Chief finally said. "I don't figure as how you're going to need to get Mrs. Mason a divorce." Clyde leaned forward and put his hands on his knees. He was listening closely now. So was I for that matter.

"Oh?" I said.

"Seeing as how Mr. Mason is no longer among us."

"Chief, what are you talking about?" I snatched up the receiver. My voice went up a half octave. Now I was leaning forward too. My hand hurt I was gripping the phone so hard.

"Drove his big car right off a cliff up around Avila Beach.

Pretty well burned up everything. We were lucky to find your card. Traced the license plate to Mason."

"So you're not sure it was him in the car?" I scratched "accident" on the pad, then "fire" and held it up for Clyde.

"Nope. Seein' as how he wasn't wearing his seat belt. Got thrown clear. Came down on the rocks. Pretty broken up. It's dangerous not wearing your seat belt." Also dangerous getting burned to death in your car, I added to myself.

"How can you be sure it was Mason? I mean, if he came down on the rocks."

"Pretty sure. Face wasn't hurt too bad."

"Someone identified the body?"

"We got hold of one of his people at the hotel he was staying at. Said it was him." Once you got the Chief going, he was a fount of information.

"How did the accident occur?"

"Not sure it was an accident."

My head shot up. "What do you mean?"

"Have to be looked at like any unexplained death."

"So, there's no reason to believe it wasn't an accident?" I swallowed. My mouth was so dry I thought I might never swallow again.

"Nope."

"Then there's nothing to worry about." I leaned back in my chair again.

"Man's dead, he's dead. Not going to worry."

Funny, I wasn't thinking about Guy Mason. "Does Mrs. Mason know?"

"Not yet. Wanted to talk to you first. Curious about your card being in the car." Maybe he thought I was a murderer. That would be bad for business. If I had been though, I would've confessed under his shrewd questioning.

"You going to call her?" I said.

"Intend to. Soon as I clear up some loose ends."

"Do you want me to call her for you?"

"Nope. Got to call her myself. But you do what you want."

I hung up. Clyde and I sat still for a few moments.

"Well," I said to Clyde. "what do you say to a woman who's just lost her husband? One who's in the process of divorcing him? 'Janet, I have terrible news'." Clyde shook his head.

Maybe not.

Chapter 34

"How'd she take the news?" Karen said. It was maybe eight hours since we had learned of Guy Mason's death.

We were at Mario's, our little Italian place in Arroyo Grande, for dinner. Sitting at a small corner table in the back. A candle was flickering. But the red checked tablecloths and the candlelight weren't having their usual happy effect.

I had an O'Doul's in my hand. It was shaking. My hand I mean. I hoped Karen hadn't noticed. I lifted the O'Doul's up to my lips and was about to take a sip when Mario came out of the kitchen and saw us. He walked over and spread his arms. I put the bottle back on the table.

"Hey, my friend Jimmy." He turned on one foot with the drama that only an Italian can muster, and opened his arms. "And my beautiful Karen."

Karen lit up. She always does when she sees Mario. He took both her hands in his.

Mario's a short, broad kind of guy with thinning gray hair and a great smile. The little wire glasses he wears down on the tip of his nose gives him a jolly, old-country look. He was wearing an apron over his dark pants and white shirt. Mario reluctantly let go of Karen and turned his attention to me.

"You want to try something, Jimmy?

"Sure." I would have tried skydiving at the moment. I really didn't want to get into the discussion I knew Karen and I were going to have about Guy Mason.

"Beer guy come by today. He want to sell me some special imported beer. He left a few bottles."

"Thanks, Mario, but you know I don't drink the alcoholic stuff anymore."

"Sure, yeah. I know. He give me a non-alcoholic beer too." Mario went over behind the bar and fooled around for a minute. Then he came back holding a cold bottle of beer. He popped the cap. "You try this. If you like it, maybe I buy some."

I held the bottle up close to my face to read the label in the dark. "Hakke Beck." I took a sip. "Hey, that's good," I said. I took another sip. "Real good. I'll drink this stuff anytime." I turned the bottle appreciatively, looking at it in the candlelight.

"Well, you have that one," Mario said ambling away. He looked back over his shoulder. "My compliments." I think he likes Karen. So do I.

I turned back to her. "That was nice of Mario. I bet he asked especially for this beer."

She nodded, then repeated her question. She's not easily distracted.

"How did Janet Mason take the news?"

"That's a little difficult to answer."

"How so?"

"She didn't seem to react at first. Maybe she was in shock. Then she became unglued. She must have loved the guy on some level, I guess."

"Or she was putting on an act."

"Yeah, there's that. It crossed my mind."

I had known some actors during my years in L.A. They were the best people and the worst people I had ever met in my life. The only problem was, I couldn't tell the difference between them. I'm not sure they could either.

Maria, Mario's wife, put down two plates of veal scaloppini in front of us. "Enjoy," she said, raising her fingers to the sky.

It smelled great. I dug in. Maria lingered until I took the first bite and nodded approvingly. Karen ignored her food. Women.

"Do you think Guy Mason's death was an accident?"

I swallowed. "Good God, I hope so." I really, really did. "There's nothing to say it wasn't." I added that last bit for Karen's sake.

I mean, I take a killer deposition but the defendants usually wait to die until after I finish. I didn't even want to think about the alternative. But, I was. And so was Karen.

"Did Janet had anything to do with her husband's death?"

That stopped my fork halfway to my lips. It was a question that hadn't occurred to me.

"You mean other than being such a bitch it drove him to commit suicide?" I gave her my best smile and continued eating.

"Jimmy, I'm serious." Her mouth was set. Her intense green eyes pinned me to my chair. My humor, if you could call it that, wasn't going to fly. I settled back further into my seat and lowered my eyes to the table. I cut another bite of scaloppini and chewed it slowly. I needed a moment to try to put things together.

"No," I said finally. I raised my head and shook it. "I don't see what she would have to gain. It doesn't make any sense. She won't get any alimony now. There's nothing in the estate according to Tony Thompson. Mason didn't even have any assets he could mortgage to finance the Franklin Farms project. That's why he has all the funny financing."

I paused and let that sink in. "No," I repeated. She hadn't asked me about Gino Bartoletti. He was the one who was worrying me.

I was putting on a good show for Karen. At least I thought so. But my hands weren't playing the same game. This conversation was making me nervous. I played with the fork. Then I played with my beer bottle. Then I knocked over my glass of water and spilled it all over the table.

Karen was watching me closely. She knows me too well. She leaned over and laid her hand over mine and stilled it.

"Don't be worried." Right. I was worried sick. I didn't like what I was thinking and I was scared. For Karen too.

I had trouble keeping my hand still when she moved hers away. I was consciously willing my hands to stay quiet. I looked enviously at Karen's glass of white wine. Karen caught the look and frowned. She gave a sharp little shake of her head. The stress was beginning to get to me. Hell, it had already gotten to me. Big-time.

Karen moved her hand down her cheek. Then she looked directly at me. She straightened. I could see the muscles in her jaw tense up.

"What does this do to us?" she said. "This death. You know, about getting out of the case? We've got to get out." Her voice had a hard edge.

"I'm with you. I'm not sticking around a minute longer than we have to. I don't like people having accidents in my cases."

"So?" She rearranged her napkin in her lap. Her food had gotten cold. Maria was giving her a concerned look from across the room.

I made it up as I went along. "Guy Mason is dead. The divorce case is over. I'll go up tomorrow and give the widow my condolences and wrap up our representation. It's simple." It always is with me.

"Does she have to sign anything?"

"I don't know. I don't think so." I caught myself. "Well, maybe she does. She'll have to relieve us. There's no death certificate yet. I can't get the court to do it. I'll get Clyde to draw up something first thing."

"What if she won't sign?"

"I can't see any reason she wouldn't. It'll just cost her money to keep going. And there's no reason." I'm an optimist. "I'll call her tomorrow morning and set up an appointment."

Karen lost her concentration. She was looking over my shoulder.

"Well, speak of the devil," she said. She raised her head and pointed her chin towards the door.

"Huh?"

"The grieving widow seems to be out drowning her sorrows."

I moved around in my seat. There was Janet in a low-cut, lemon yellow dress, coming through the door, displaying a dazzling flash of cleavage. She had turned her head to speak to someone. My friend Gino came in behind her, dressed all in black. They made a handsome couple. Heads turned at their entrance. He said something that made her smile. They laughed, looking at each other.

I waved. Funny, they didn't wave back.

Chapter 35

I couldn't see her eyes. Given the size of her knitted bikini, I could see almost everything else. She was lying by the pool when I came around the corner of the house. A yellow towel covered the chaise lounge under her.

A spent bottle of Dom Perignon lay on its side. She had her brunette hair tied up in a ponytail that stuck out the back of the dark blue baseball cap she was wearing. The cap said "Desperate Shop Girls" in large red letters.

Where in the world could you sit by the pool in March? Okay, global warming. But come on.

As I said, I couldn't see her eyes. She had on these big dark sunglasses. But, I could see her mouth. That wasn't pretty. Maybe I was reading something into it I shouldn't.

I had checked the driveway before I came in. No gray Mercedes. No Gino Bartoletti. No fireplug. That made me feel better.

"Good morning, Janet," I said as I walked up to the pool. My voice was mellifluous. "I waved to you last night at Mario's." Janet ignored my comment.

She looked up from the paperback book she was reading. I arched my neck to see the author. Barbara Taylor.

"I'm using the name Sullivan now," she said. A non sequitur. It was okay with me. Whatever. She fished a bookmark out of the book and laid the book on the small table beside the chaise lounge.

I sat down on the other chaise lounge. I was facing her with the sun warming my back. There was a soft breeze. It blew my hair forward into my eyes. I brushed it away. The view over the ocean up here was breathtaking. I could smell the new cut grass and cattle on the surrounding acreage.

"I'm sorry about the death of your husband." Given last night, I might be the only one here who was sorry, but I thought I should say it. It turned out I shouldn't have. She snorted.

"That pig."

Okay again. For my next act –- "I feel badly about your case. Now you won't get the alimony. I know there's nothing in the estate."

That brought outright laughter. Some laughter is more frightening than a scream. Whatever was going on, I wasn't at the party. She actually clapped her hands. Her mouth tightened.

"You're a complete idiot," she said.

Well, a half-wit, maybe. Not a complete idiot. I resented the remark. But I was committed to playing nice. "What do you mean?"

"Do you think I could live on $100,000 a year?" I thought she was drunk. A mean drunk at that.

"Well, I know it's not a lot of money . . ." I didn't believe those words had just come out of my mouth, "but it would help. Now there's nothing."

There was that laugh again. The ponytail bobbed with it. What the hell was going on?

"You don't worry about me, Jimmy boy, I'll be just fine." Maybe she was so distraught she'd taken to drinking. Poor woman.

"I'm the only beneficiary of the estate," she said. "What do they call it? The sole surviving heir."

"I don't get it."

"You wouldn't." A sarcastic tone. And here I was the attorney she couldn't go on without just a few days ago.

"Help me," I said.

"I'm going to be rich." She was bragging now.

"You mean because of the Franklin Farms development?"

"You're kidding, right?"

"No, not really." It's true I was fishing. But I wasn't kidding.

"The estate is agreeing to a foreclosure on this property." She waved her hand around carelessly. Her movements were loose and choppy. Then she leaned forward a little unsteadily and looked around her with an air of disgust. "It was a lousy idea to start with." She stopped. A little smile played at the corner of her lips. "But it had its uses."

How did she know the estate was agreeing to be foreclosed out of the project the day after Guy Mason's death? How could she . . . how could the estate . . . have made the analysis of the economics that quickly? What did she mean by "It had its uses."? I was lost. It wasn't the first time.

"But there won't be anything left," I said.

"Oh, you're exactly right, Jimmy." Her lips turned up in a sneer. "Except, of course, for the $5,000,000 of insurance."

I could only nod. I let it ripen a moment. In the silence I was aware of the small sound the filter flap makes as it works in the pool.

"I don't need you any more," she said. I want you out. Now."

So much for gratitude.

"You're sure?" My God, What was I saying. I could bite my tongue but that's permanent disability for a lawyer.

"I've got the best estate lawyer in Los Angeles. What would I need you for?" This woman was a quick worker.

That's where I wanted to be anyway. Great. Right?

"Look you'll have to sign a dismissal of the divorce case and a release for the firm. I brought the papers with me."

She looked at me and didn't say a word. Her lips were two thin red lines. She just held out her hand. I passed her the two sheets of paper and the Bic pen I always carry.

"You need to sign there . . ." I pointed to the signature line on the first form. Then I turned the page to the release that Clyde had prepared and pointed to the bottom. "And there." She scrawled her name on both documents and shoved the papers back at me.

"Thanks," I said. "It was a pleasure representing you." Leave 'em smiling I always say. I got to my feet and turned to leave.

"Hey. Wait a minute."

I turned back with a query on my face.

"Where're the papers to dismiss the Franklin Farms lawsuit?"

"You're not the client," I said. You can't dismiss it." I must admit, it gave me a little frisson of pleasure to hit her with that.

"What do you mean, I'm not the client? I'm paying you, damn it." Her voice carried an ugly overtone with it.

"Susie Wilson's the client." I didn't mention SOC. What was the point? "That's what you wanted, remember?"

For a moment I thought I saw panic in her face. Its hard to tell. I wish I could have seen her eyes. Her mouth tightened. And I thought her body stiffened.

"Get out of here," she said.

I did.

Chapter 36

"Tony," I said, tapping the eraser of my pencil on the top of my desk, "you told me there were no assets in the estate." I was on the phone with Tony Thompson. His was the first call I made when I reached my office. I hadn't even bothered to take off my sports coat.

Bruno was lying in his usual position on the couch. He raised his head up off his paws and gave me a peculiar look. I guess my voice sounded funny. I wouldn't doubt it.

"No," Tony said.

"What do you mean 'no'? You said there were no assets." I pulled down my tie.

"No."

"Yes you did."

"No. I said there was no value in any assets that Mason could mortgage."

"Isn't that what I just said?"

"No."

"Quit saying that."

"Yes." "Damn it Tony, are you trying to drive me nuts?"

He started giggling. Maybe he was too far into tax season.

"Jimmy, there are all kinds of assets that don't have a value but can still be valuable." There was a little bubble of laughter. I was glad Tony was having a good time. I was just sorry I couldn't get my hands around his neck.

"Huh?" I said. I like to be incisive.

"Sure."

"Like insurance, you mean?" I put down my pencil and got up. I started to pace, tethered by the phone cord.

"Good guess," Tony said.

"How can that be? Insurance costs a lot of money."

"Well, with insurance the answer is yes and no." Here we go again.

"Look, why don't I quit asking you questions and you just tell me the answers."

"Okay. Here it is. If life insurance is whole life, it has an asset value you can borrow against. But it's very expensive.

If you want cheap insurance, you buy term. Usually guaranteed level payment term."

Sure, just what I would do. I had no idea what Tony was talking about.

"It costs a lot less because it doesn't build up any cash value. In other words, it's not worth anything unless you die."

"Don't tell me. Guy Mason had term insurance," I said. I was walking in a little circle to keep the phone cord from tugging the phone off the desk. The carpet was starting to complain.

"I did tell you. That's exactly what I said when we were preparing for the deposition. Don't you remember?"

"No." My turn.

"Well, I did."

"I believe you."

"What difference does it make?" Tony asked.

"I don't know yet." I came to a stop. Bruno looked up. I ignored him. He put his head back down on his paws. "Anyway, thanks."

I sat down and hung up. My mind was churning. This wasn't good.

That's when Clyde interrupted me and threw me off track.

"Hey, boss. You ready to go?"

The short answer was "No", since I had no plans to go anywhere. So, I gave him my most lawyer-like response. "Where'd you have in mind?"

He looked at me like I was off my rocker. It wasn't too far off the mark. Clyde was dressed in a suit and tie. He cleans up well.

"The contempt hearing in the Jenkins case," he said. "You remember." He glanced at his watch. "We gotta go right now or we'll be late."

It had completely slipped my mind.

He waved a folder at me. "I've got copies of the pleadings right here. I'll drive. You can review them on the way. Oh, you better comb your hair."

I grabbed my briefcase and we headed out to his car. No lawyer shows up in court without a briefcase. Even if it's empty. Mine was.

Hail the conquering hero. Another victory for the great Jimmy Harris. Clarence Jenkins had been socked with sanctions. Judge Anderson told Clarence, in no uncertain terms, he'd get his ass thrown in jail if he didn't pay the child support ordered by the court. And pay it on time.

I think Clarence got the idea he didn't want to be in front of Judge Anderson again. On the other hand, based on the look he gave me on the way out, I didn't believe he liked me very much anymore. Given how much he liked me before the hearing, I thought maybe I better do something.

"Mr. Jenkins," I called out. He turned and gave me a cold look. I have a lot of experience with cold looks. I walked up to him and held out my hand. "I'm sorry about all this fuss. No hard feelings. It's not personal."

He gave my hand a look like I was extending a water snake for him to take hold of and turned on his heel. I got the feeling I hadn't completely charmed him. I'd have to keep my eyes peeled.

To keep your eyes peeled, which seems like it would hurt a lot, is actually derived from the Latin word for pillage or plunder. I was more worried about being on the receiving end. Clarence had a gun.

Clyde got talkative on the way back to San Buenasera. He gets that way after a hearing sometimes. If we win.

"You're sure good, boss." He turned in his seat to look over at me. I wanted him to keep his eyes on the road. We were doing 85. Clyde tends to drive a little erratically and I wanted to be alive so my other fans could have their shot. Also, I was leaving finger marks in his dashboard.

"The way you got the judge to give us the sanctions. I thought Jenkins' lawyer was going to have a fit."

I gave him my patented toothy smile. "Thanks. It's all my years of experience. I hope you were paying attention." My statement had the impact I had come to expect.

"Absolutely, boss. Sure thing. I took notes." Clyde turned back to look at the highway and swerved around a Ferrari that was only doing 80. The Ferrari driver made a motion at us with his middle finger I didn't quite catch.

"We may have some trouble collecting," I said.

"Oh, yeah. That'll be the fun part," Clyde said. Little did he know. Hell, little did I know.

We made it back to the office alive. That's more of an accomplishment than it sounds like. You weren't riding with Clyde.

Karen poked her head out of her office as we walked in. She was holding on to the doorjamb with one hand and leaning through the door. She looked great.

"How did it go with Janet?"

We hadn't had a chance to talk since I got back this morning, what with my phone call to Tony and Clyde rushing me out.

"Sullivan." I said.

"What?"

"Janet want's to use her stage name again."

"So? Did she sign the papers?"

"Yeah."

"We're okay then."

"Sure." Why worry her? "I'll tell you all about it at dinner. I've got some stuff I need to get done right now," I said, motioning professionally at my office door. She didn't seem satisfied, but I didn't know where to take it yet. I went into my office and tossed my coat on the couch. Bruno registered his distress at the usurpation of his space.

Bruno momentarily struggled to a standing position and then curled himself up on my coat. He gave me a look. Then he put his muzzle back down on his paws and started making soft snoring sounds. The dog leads a tough life.

My answering machine was giving me its angry red eye. I went over and punched the message button. It was Susie Wilson's voice.

"Jimmy, you have to call me right away." She sounded scared.

Chapter 37

"You're kidding."

Pamela and I were alone in the office. I mean I had been in my office and Pamela had been sitting behind her desk in the reception area. It was 9:30 the next morning. Far too early for me to be at the top of my game.

And this was a wake-me-up if I'd ever had one. I was now standing in the reception room next to Pamela's desk in response to her nervous summons.

"No, Mr. Harris. I'm not." The man standing in front of me was dressed in a dark suit, a white shirt and a boring tie. His thin dark hair was graying at the temples. The black shoes he wore had the best polish I'd seen since the Army. He reached into his inner pocket and took out a small folded leather case. He held it up by his cheek and let it drop open, just like you see in the movies.

"Special Agent Walter Leary of the Federal Bureau of Investigation."

"Right. What can I do for you?" Holy shit. I'd never seen an FBI agent in the flesh before, much less had one standing in front of me. Tall, square jaw. Maybe late forties or early fifties. He looked like Dick Tracy.

I quickly reviewed my past life to make sure there were no federal offenses I'd committed for which the statute of limitations hadn't run. Check. I tried to suppress my overwhelming urge to surrender and confess anyway.

He reached into the other side of his jacket and pulled out a sheet of paper folded lengthwise. "I have a subpoena here for all of the financial records of a Mr. Guy Mason." He handed it to me.

I was blindsided. I didn't know what to say. I opened the subpoena and scanned it. "Uh . . ." He waited, looking at me. "Uh . . ." Really articulate. One more "uh" and I'd hold the California "uh" record for a lawyer before noon. "I'm worried about privilege," I said.

I amused him. "Come on, Mr. Harris, there's no privilege. These are documents you got from a third party. I'm a lawyer too." I remembered. Lot's of FBI agents were lawyers.

And he was right. "Why are you subpoenaing them from me? Why not Guy Mason?" Apart from the fact that he was dead.

"His estate's in formation. There's no one to serve. We wanted to proceed expeditiously." He gave me his official smile. I'm sure they have a special class at the Academy for smiling. One for witnesses, one for perps. And one for dumb-ass lawyers trying to stall for time. "You've done our work for us," he said. He said it without rearranging his smile. Probably a separate lesson.

Leary glanced down at Bruno, who had deigned to join us. Bruno's tongue lolled out as he gazed up at him, wagging his tail like mad. The traitor.

"Nice dog," Leary said. He bent down to scratch Bruno's ear.

I ignored him. "How'd you know I had Guy Mason's financial records?"

"Mr. Harris," he said, looking up into my face, "we're not called the Federal Bureau of Investigation for nothing. This wasn't too hard." He stood back up.

I was running out of questions. I looked at the subpoena again. It seemed to be in order. Then I focused on the case name. The United States v. The United Union Pension Fund. Gino Bartoletti. Yikes.

"Can you give me an hour or two to consult with my colleagues?" I said. It would take me that long to find some colleagues. "Of course, we want to co-operate fully with the

FBI," I said. I didn't break into the "Stars and Stripes Forever". I wanted to. "I just have to make sure we're following all of our ethical constraints."

"Naturally, Mr. Harris." I don't think I fooled him. "I'll call you back in a few hours so we can arrange to pick up the files."

"We'll need to make copies." That would give us a day or two. I said it quickly. Maybe too quickly.

"We'll make a full copy and return it to you."

Right. If you can't trust your Federal government, who can you trust? He did a parade ground about face and marched out the door.

Gino Bartoletti. He wasn't going to be pleased with me when I turned over those files. Somehow, I didn't think he'd be too impressed with the majesty of a subpoena. This must be part of the pension fund investigation I'd read about in the New York Times. Maybe.

Was there anything in the files that referred to Bartoletti or the United Union Pension Fund? I had no idea. Tony Thompson had reviewed the files. I better call him.

This was becoming a very stressful day. Susie Wilson hadn't answered her phone at the hair salon this morning. Or at home. I had taken the Jaguar and swung by her shop. It was locked up tight.

I looked over at Pamela. She was sitting there wide-eyed. She hadn't moved a muscle while I was talking to Mr. Leary. She would probably tell this story to her grandchildren. Right now I was concerned about her telling the story to more current folks.

"Pamela," I said.

"Yes, Jimmy," like I woke her up.

"Let's keep this to ourselves. It's really important this remains between us. Okay?"

Her head bobbed up and down.

"Good." Really good if I didn't want to have another conference with Mr. Bartoletti or his minion. My face throbbed at the memory.

I gave her a smile that said "I trust you completely", crossed my fingers behind my back and went into my office. Things were just great.

Last night Karen and I had talked about my visit with Janet and my discussion with Tony. She hadn't hesitated to point out to me the fallacy in my analysis. The one about why Janet wasn't involved that I so brilliantly put forth at Mario's. There were now 5,000,000 reasons Janet would want Guyboy to depart this world. And it would also make sense out of her turning a $2,000,000 settlement offer down flat. If, of course, she had reasons to suspect her hubby was near death.

I sat at my desk, tapping on it with my fingers, trying to think this through. Okay, so here I was. My client Susie Wilson was scared shitless, judging by her voice on my answering machine. Now she was nowhere to be found.

Maybe she was in hiding. Maybe worse, God forbid. I had to figure it had something to do with the Franklin Farms lawsuit and that lawsuit had something to do with Janet. Janet now Sullivan had looked terrified when I told her she couldn't dismiss the lawsuit. I think I even mentioned Susie's name.

Janet wanted her husband dead. Gino had something going with Janet. Gino was not a nice man. He might be the one behind the offshore financing of the Franklin Farms project.

The financing was now being foreclosed. The property would be more valuable with vested entitlements, the rights granted by the City Council to build all those houses. The rights Susie Wilson's lawsuit was standing in the way of. The rights I was also standing in the way of.

The FBI seemed to be interested in Mr. Bartoletti and his employer. Mr. Bartoletti was intent on not having his name associated with Franklin Farms, as he had explained to me persuasively. And I was sure he was interested in staying out of jail. Just a wild guess. I was getting a puckering feeling in my nether regions.

I still had no idea what was going on. But here and there, I was starting to connect the pixels. The pixels weren't making a pretty picture.

I needed to make sure the picture didn't end up being blood red. I hate the sight of blood. Particularly my own. That's why I became a lawyer instead of a doctor. Forgetting, for the moment, I wasn't bright enough to become a doctor.

I had a couple of hours before the FBI contacted me again. The smart thing to do was to try to find Susie and get the hell out of the Franklin Farms lawsuit. I needed her signature, and I needed her to get a signature from Save Our Coast. Maybe I could get out of Gino's way. It seemed like a good idea.

There was no reason for him to know the FBI got the files from me. Right?

That's when I heard a crack like a gunshot. I must have jumped a foot. Then I dropped to the floor and covered my head.

Bruno jumped down off the couch. He waddled over and started licking my face. He loves it when I get down on the floor and play with him. Today I was playing dead. "No, Bruno," I said. I put my arm around him and drew him in to my side. He made himself comfortable. We laid there together.

A minute or maybe two went by. Nothing else happened. No more cracks. No tinkle of glass. No horrible screams.

I got to my knees and crawled over towards the window. Keeping low, I slowly got to my feet. I stuck close to the wall and looked cautiously out the side window. I could just see the Jaguar in the driveway. The front and back windows had been blown out.

Great. Now my problems had problems.

Chapter 38

"How are you doing?" Karen asked. Her voice was muffled.

We were lying in bed. Our bedroom had a muzzy gray feeling. It was that special time of morning, not still dark and not quite light, when the newspapers come. She had her head on my chest. Her hand was on my arm.

Her breath was tickling my chest hairs. I shifted slightly and looked down at the top of her head. It was messed in a sleepy, cute way. I could see a pillow mark creasing her cheek.

Normally in this position I'm doing just hunky dory. It's nice to be warm and naked with Karen. This morning I felt like a canary at a cat convention.

She lifted up a little and arched her back. Then she stretched out one arm up over her head, turning a bit. The motion was slow and languid and ended in a yawn. I could almost hear her purr. Finally she settled down again onto my chest. I marvel at the grace of women. My woman.

"Are you worried about the FBI?" Neither of us had slept that well, skittering along the edge of consciousness. It had been two days since the FBI picked up the Guy Mason files. We still hadn't gotten any copies.

"Not so much that. More about Susie." We hadn't been able to find her. No one knew where she was. Karen had called several of her customers to see if they had been given any hint. No one knew a thing.

"I'd just like to be out of this case. Particularly with the FBI involved," I said, smoothing a strand of her hair "Someone's not going to be happy about what's going on." I already wasn't.

"Did you speak to Mike?" Mike runs our one and only local garage. Lately he'd been seeing even more of the Jaguar than usual. After I'd swept out all the broken glass from the windshield, that's where I had taken the car. The only one who was pleased about the windows was Bruno. He didn't have to lean out to have the wind blow on his ears.

"Mike said the car would be ready this afternoon. Maybe we'll walk over after work and pick it up."

"Is there anything we can do about Clarence Jenkins?" The Jaguar and Clarence were becoming wedded in our mind. It must be Pavlovian. She raised her head and her eyes found me. I saw the small universe of freckles that swept over her nose.

I think she's worried about me. I can't blame her. So am I. Besides, we have the kid to protect. As if on cue, Bruno gave a snort and rolled over at the end of the bed.

"I just don't know. When Chief Carsone was out at the office, he didn't seem hopeful." Hope was pretty much his strong suit. I had called the good chief first thing after I saw someone had shot out the car windows. It had taken him an hour to break free. Even I wouldn't want his coffee to get cold. "No one saw anything. There's no way to charge anybody," he had stated with assurance.

"But it's got to be Clarence. Something like this happens every time you take him to court," Karen said.

"You know it. And I know it. But it's all circumstantial. They can't do anything. Maybe we should hire somebody to watch him."

"Jimmy, we can't afford that."

"I know." I said it with a sigh. "Even if we could, it might take forever." She snuggled up against me and gave me a hug. She still had a lingering scent of soap from her evening shower.

"It'll be okay. It's only a car." The car. But who's counting.

"Don't forget the office window," I said.

She punched me playfully. "You know what I mean.

"Yeah. You're right." On the other hand, our insurance agent is beginning to age noticeably.

She snuggled in close again. Even in my subdued state I can't resist a naked beautiful woman. Not one I loved. I nudged Bruno off the bed with my toe.

Karen looked up. What's that?"

"Nothing."

My hand found her sweet spot and started doing its job.

"Umm," she said.

Then I did my "Umm".

It took about an hour before we rolled out of bed and showered. We were on foot so we put Bruno on the leash and headed up the hill to the Lilly Pad for breakfast.

It must've been ten before we finally made it into the office. It was whistling weather and we were holding hands when we walked in.

"Good morning, Pamela," I said. I took the stack of mail that Pamela was holding out for me.

"Morning, Jimmy. Morning, Karen." She smiled at us. Pamela does that in the morning. I'll have to try it sometime.

Bruno and I went into our office. By the time I sat down, Bruno had settled onto the couch for his morning nap.

I started through the mail. Bill. I pulled out the right hand drawer. Pleadings. I made a pile for Clyde.

But I was on my feet as I confronted the next item. A dismissal with prejudice of the Franklin Farms lawsuit signed by Susie Wilson. It had a handwritten note attached to the top by a paperclip.

"Karen," I shouted as I headed for the door. We nearly bumped into each other as she came through the doorway.

"Look at this," I said, holding out the note and release. We retreated back into my office.

I stood over Karen's shoulder as she read the note.

No lawsuit's worth getting killed for.

I've skipped. I don't know if I'll be back.

Those people have me terrified.

Take me out of this lawsuit. I'm sorry. Susie.

It looked like she'd written the note in haste. Who were "those people"? Janet? Gino? Someone else? There were lots of unhappy choices.

Now what was I supposed to do? Susie was gone. But I still had a lawsuit and a client. Save Our Coast. Only I had no idea who the client was. Susie had always dealt with them. I didn't even know where they were.

With Susie gone "those people" were going to expect the lawsuit to go away. "Those people" terrified Susie. Guess who was going to be next.

"Clyde," I yelled. "Pamela."

Clyde and Pamela hurried in. I don't think they've ever heard me yell like that. Even Bruno jumped. Karen had a "deer in the headlights" look.

"Pamela, where's the envelope for this letter?" I waved the release in the air.

"I don't know, Jimmy. I must have thrown it away when I sorted the mail. Like I usually do." She looked flustered. She was rubbing her pudgy little hands together.

"It's all right. Go through your trash can. This is really important. The envelope's probably hand-addressed. See if you can find it."

"Okay."

I turned to Clyde and handed him the release and the note. He skimmed them. "No SOC." Clyde got it in one. Smart fellow.

"Can you go into the on-line not-for-profit data base and see if you can pull up their filings? We need their address and an officers list." We needed an officer to sign the dismissal. "As soon as you can."

Pamela was back holding an envelope. She handed it to Karen.

"The postmark is San Buenasera," Karen said. "Damn. She must have sent it before she left." No help.

"Clyde?"

But he was already halfway out the door.

Chapter 39

"Mr. Harris, this is Special Agent Leary of the FBI."

It was cold in my office. I had been warming my hands around a cup of coffee and wondering how Clyde was doing. We needed someone at Save Our Coast who could sign our consent. I figured with everyone else out of the lawsuit, SOC wouldn't want to pay the bills. At least not mine.

At worst, I figured I could still get out of the lawsuit. I'm sure there was some young, selfless pro bono lawyer who would sacrifice himself in this cause. Or herself. I'm politically correct. Maybe sacrifice himself –- or herself --, literally. Then the phone rang and things went south.

A call from the FBI wasn't my idea of how to start the morning. I hoped for the best. "Hi, Special Agent Leary. Are my files ready?"

It was a bellicose day. I mean weatherwise. The wind was blowing. It must have been 59 or 60 degrees out. A low-pressure system was moving in. That's the way it is on the

Central Coast in winter. One day it's great and the next, it's great, but different.

"This isn't about the files."

I felt a tsunami of a headache coming on. My hopes of tying this matter up in a nice little bundle and depositing it on someone else's doorstep were rapidly shredding.

I turned in my chair and looked longingly out over the harbor. It had been a long, long time. Somewhere out there a boat needed my attention. Somewhere naked breasts were bobbing unwatched. Somewhere men are laughing. Somewhere children shout. A melancholy took me.

"Oh," I said. These things trip off my tongue.

"I'd like to make an appointment to come out and see you," Leary said. I felt the wind rattling my windows like somebody was rattling my cage.

"As much as I'd enjoy that, I'm real busy right now."

"Mr. Harris, perhaps I haven't made myself clear. I'm conducting a criminal investigation. It wasn't a request. I can get a subpoena."

"Right. How about tomorrow?" Hope springs eternal. There's an old saying I live by. "He who puts off until tomorrow what he can do today will eventually get out of doing one day's work."

"How about today?"

"Can you give me some idea of what you need so I can see if I can fit it into my schedule?" My pencil hovered over my empty life.

"I want to talk to you about Gino Bartoletti."

I broke it into two pretty yellow pieces. I'm hell on pencils.

"I don't know much about Mr. Bartoletti," I said. I tried for a cheery, helpful voice. "I've only met him a couple of times. I'm not sure there's much I can tell you." Funny, it had gotten warmer in here.

"Let me be the judge of that. You may be surprised."

"I can give you an hour at around four." I didn't have my heart in it.

He didn't seem to care. "See you then."

"When . . . ?" But he had hung up.

"Clyde," I called out.

"Boss, you're not going to like this." Clyde had laid a sheath of printouts on my desk. He was leaning over them looking for one. He was right. I didn't like it already.

I closed my eyes and leaned my head against my chair. I pushed back and ran my hand through my hair. I've been doing that so much lately, I'm surprised there's any left. No wonder it was thinning. "Tell me," I said to the ceiling.

"You remember how I mentioned Susie Wilson was having trouble getting the complaint signed because Save Our Coast was reorganizing?"

"No. So what?"

"Well, I guess it reorganized."

"Clyde, would you get to the point. I may be too old to care otherwise."

"Susie Wilson is now President."

"Shit. You know she's gone. Who's the Vice President?"

"There isn't one."

"What do you mean. There must be." I bumped forward. "It's required by law. At least a Secretary is. Who's the Secretary?"

"Susie Wilson's the only officer listed on the form. The address of SOC has been changed to her shop in town."

"Wonderful," I said. I moved my hand over my face trying to get some blood circulating. That old tag line from the

"Life of Riley" ran through my mind. "What a revoltin' development this is."

Now I'd have to publish notice to serve SOC. It would take me a month to get to court to ask to be relieved in the Franklin Farms case. And who knew what the court would do. I could see myself explaining all this to Gino Bartoletti and how very understanding he would be.

"The good news is I filed the motion for us to collect the sanctions in the Jenkins matter," Clyde said. "It'll be heard next week."

That was the good news! Lord help us.

It was four o'clock. No matter how much you may wish otherwise, four o'clock occurs around the same time every afternoon.

"Special Agent Leary is here," Pamela said in a slightly awed voice. Every FBI agent is special.

"Why don't you show him in." I didn't figure he'd go away.

I stood. Agent Leary was wearing a dark blue suit and a white shirt. I could still see my face in his shoes. He had on a red, white and blue striped tie. I guess today must be a holiday.

I held out my hand and we shook. "Would you like some coffee or a cold drink?"

"No." He settled into my client chair. "Thank you for seeing me, Mr. Harris." As if I had a choice. "This will be an informal discussion. You are not under oath." Damn straight. "But I would remind you that lying to an FBI agent can be a federal offense."

That was nice. Now I felt much more comfortable.

"I don't want to take too much of your time." He took out a small notebook and clicked his ballpoint pen. "Tell me what you know of the relationship between Janet Mason and Gino Bartoletti."

Jeez, not even any foreplay. And here I was about to get screwed.

"I've seen them together at dinner. That's all." Maybe my voice rose a little. This was a grave discussion to me. I mean that literally. I didn't volunteer the Mercedes parked up at the Farm. I never saw Gino up there. Felt him, maybe. Saw him, no. I didn't think Mr. Bartoletti would be pleased with me gossiping about his love life to the FBI.

Special Agent Leary brushed away my answer with a couple of short flicks of the back of his hand. He looked up at me. I didn't like the look in his eyes. His mouth was firm. "We know all about Mr. Bartoletti's affair with Mrs. Mason.

That's well established. What we're interested in are their business affairs."

Business affairs? I didn't squirm. Squirming requires intent. No. Maybe I moved a little in my seat. To get more comfortable. No squirming, see. "I'm sorry. What do you mean?"

"I mean what we're trying to determine is their business relationship in the Franklin Farms project." He looked hard at me as he spoke. The hair on the back of my neck levitated.

"I don't know anything about that."

I blurted that out. Was the information privileged even though I didn't have any information?

He leaned forward, straining the lovely crease in his trousers There was something aggressive about the way he sat on the edge of the chair. "We have telephone transcripts of Mrs. Mason telling Mr. Bartoletti that you were subpoenaing documents that could be embarrassing to them. She suggested he speak to you. We want to know what that was all about. What did you and Mr. Bartoletti discuss?"

I rubbed my eye. The one that had finally become a reasonably normal skin color again. I liked it that way. I looked at Special Agent Leary. He looked back. The calm look on his face scared the hell out of me. What was I going to say? What could I say that would keep me out of jail? As well as free of Mr. Bartoletti's displeasure?

"Gosh," --gosh?--, he just didn't want his name associated with Franklin Farms. I thought he didn't want Guy Mason to know."

"So, you're not aware that Bartoletti financed the Franklin Farms project?"

"No." Thought it. Didn't know it.

"Or that Janet Mason has agreed to allow him to foreclose immediately."

"She mentioned something to me about the foreclosure. I didn't know anything else about it. I had no idea who was going to foreclose. I'm just her divorce attorney." I gave him my most disarming smile. He didn't bite.

"Uh huh." His ballpoint pin clicked in and out. "Didn't that strike you as a little strange?"

"I'm just a small town lawyer. I don't know about those business things."

"Sure. I suppose you didn't know the money she paid you came from Gino Bartoletti?"

"No."

"Why do you think that was?" He sounded so innocent when he asked the question.

"I've got no idea." I really meant that.

"Mr. Harris, I'll tell you, I'm not satisfied with your answers." He snapped his notebook shut and slipped it back into his pocket. "I suggest you think long and hard about them." He clipped his pen in beside it. "I would feel badly if you were to get into a lot of trouble over something that wasn't your problem."

He reached into the other side of his coat and took out a small leather case. He withdrew a card and handed it to me. "This whole thing's a lot bigger than you think. Call me if you have anything more you want to tell me."

He got up and executed one of his parade ground turns. He didn't say goodbye.

I sat there in silence. He may have not liked my answers. I sure wasn't crazy about his questions.

Chapter 40

It was cold in San Buenasera. Around 54 degrees with an on-shore breeze. Our low-pressure system had moved in. I had my coat collar pulled up around my chin and my hands jammed into my pockets. It was freezing. I was wandering down Main Street after breakfast, window-shopping. Pussy Galore had a very artistic window display.

I hadn't slept well after my conversation with Special Agent Leary. I couldn't stop thinking about what he had said. The money Janet gave me came from Gino Bartoletti. It didn't seem to make any sense.

Okay, I could see his financing the divorce. He was getting a return on his money. But Bartoletti couldn't possibly want me to challenge the entitlements to Franklin Farms, could he? It occurred to me I had never discussed with Janet how to apply the retainers. What difference did it make?

I felt like quicksand was making a sucking sound at my feet and I would soon be drawn in over my head. Who was I kidding? I was in way over my head already. What the hell was going on?

All that was running through my mind when the big, gray Mercedes slid up to the curb behind me. Okay, so I was doing a lousy job of keeping my eyes peeled. But remember, I was keeping my eyes peeled for Clarence. I hadn't got around to adding Gino Bartoletti to the list.

The slamming of the car door made me jump. I've been a little on edge, you know. I turned my head. The sight of the fireplug walking towards me sent my scrotum into a cowardly retreat.

He pointed towards the back door of the car and jerked his head sideways. He didn't find it necessary to speak. Neither did I.

I went over to the car with the fireplug walking right behind my left elbow. He reached around me and opened the door. How very polite. I would have been impressed if I hadn't been scared out of my socks.

Baroletti did his finger crooking thing at me and then pointed down to the seat beside him. It made me think of the old joke about Italian foreplay where the guy snaps his fingers and points to his crotch. Somehow that smile didn't make it to my lips. Gino was dressed in a slub-weave, tan silk sports jacket over a black silk tee shirt and black trousers.

As I got in, Bartoletti turned back and sat staring straight ahead. The fireplug slipped in behind the wheel and the car rolled away from the curb.

Bartoletti didn't say a word. We rode in chilly silence. The traffic on the 101 was heavier than usual, but inside the car it was as quiet as a whisper. Then, as we passed Avila Beach, Bartoletti looked across at me. His eyes seemed coal black. Maybe it was the light.

"I don't like it when people make my life difficult."

I don't like people like that either and I was eager to let him see I wasn't one of those people. Incredibly eager.

"Why are you still in the Franklin Farms lawsuit?" he said. The look on his face wasn't as friendly as I would have hoped.

"Mr. Bartoletti, hasn't Janet told you how hard I'm trying to get out of it? I really am." Really, really, really. He just kept looking at me with those cold eyes.

"It's just that she wanted me to bring the case in the names of other people and I need to get them to dismiss the suit. I've been trying to reach them," I said. I was babbling. "I expect to get it cleared up in the next day or two." That was news to me.

Bartoletti turned away. He didn't seem to be listening

anymore. Then he looked at me again. "Janet had you bring the lawsuit?"

"Gee, I hope I'm not talking out of school here. That may have been privileged."

He grabbed my arm. His fingers dug into my bicep. It hurt. "Do you know who I am?"

That was a showstopper. I kept my mouth shut. It was the first smart thing I did all morning. This guy scared me up and down my spine. That was the second smart thing I did all morning.

He leaned in towards me. No more than four or five inches from my face. His eyes dug into me. He had flecks of spittle at the corner of his mouth. He tightened his grip.

"Do you have any idea what I'll do to you if you're lying to me?" His voice was very low and very calm. He had peppermint breathe. I had no idea what he was talking about.

What was this with everybody accusing me of lying. Yesterday it was Special Agent Leary, today it was Gino Bartoletti. Sure I lie. I'm a lawyer, for Christ's sake. It was my best grade in law school. I kept that to myself.

"Mr. Bartoletti, I'm not lying. I'm really trying to get out." I was answering the wrong question, but how was I to know. He shoved me away with a disgusted look on his face.

"Get rid of him," he said to the fireplug. His hand flicked me away like a piece of dirt. They pulled over to the side and I got out in a hurry. I hoped that "get rid of him" meant drop me by the side of the road. I still had my hand on the door handle when the car fishtailed away. Gravel tattooed my legs. It hurt like hell.

For the second time I went searching for a taxi after a ride with Gino Bartoletti. And looking was definitely better than being found.

Chapter 41

"Do you remember them mentioning anything about Franklin Farms, Maria? Or maybe development?" It was eleven in the morning. Mr. Bartoletti had booted me out half an hour ago. It took a few minutes to get a cab. These cab fares were killing me. I wondered if I could add it to Janet's bill. I made a mental note.

I had the cab drop me at Mario's restaurant. Maria, Mario's wife, and I were sitting at a little table. The restaurant was empty. Funny how a restaurant that looks so romantic by candlelight looks shabby in the daytime. I was hoping Maria had overheard a snatch of conversation that might give me some idea of what was going on.

Of course, I was grasping at straws. But I was a drowning man. My mind was wonderfully focused by fear, as Samuel Johnson predicted, and I was doing the only thing I could think of to do. But then again, I wasn't sure a straw could keep me afloat.

I knew Janet and Gino had eaten at Mario's, at least twice, maybe more. I also know how people talk at the table in a restaurant like they were in private. Particularly if they are into each other.

I once sat in a booth behind a lawyer preparing his client for a deposition I was about to take after breakfast. I was chewing on a bagel and taking notes. I took a great deposition, let me tell you. It happens on airplanes too. People talk like no one else is around. Go figure. .

Anyway, who else might have heard anything? But Maria was acting nervous. Her small plump hands were working the end of her apron and she wasn't meeting my eyes anymore. She's always liked me. She likes Karen even better. Everyone does. I guessed maybe she wasn't comfortable talking about her customers. That's a good thing.

I rolled out my big guns. "I know I'm asking a lot, Maria. I'm sorry. I'm just afraid Karen's in danger." Not to mention me and Bruno. "I've really got to figure out what's going on."

"You and Karen in danger?" Wow, I got included. "How is this?"

I gave her a rough sketch, not including my getting beaten up or exactly what Bartoletti said. I didn't want to get her in trouble too. "I'm trying to put all the pieces together. That's why I came to you and asked you these questions." Then I kept my mouth shut and let her process all that.

She came to her conclusion. I could see it in her face. Her jaw firmed. She wiped her hands on the end of her apron and dropped it in her lap.

"I want to help you, Jimmy. But I don't know nothing, I think." She was looking straight at me.

"Maybe not. That's okay." I gave her a smile and leaned in towards her and put my elbows on the table. My luck, it was still wet. I ignored it in a manly way.

"Let's just talk. Maybe you'll think of something." I lifted up my elbow and rubbed at my sleeve. "How many times did Ms. Mason and Mr. Bartoletti come in during the last few months?"

"Lots. Maybe ten times." Maria perked up. She likes repeat customers.

"How did they seem together?"

"That iss a little funny. Sometimes they seem like lovers. Most of the time. A few times, it was like they talk business. You know how people are when they are talking the business. I know because I do not go to a table when people are talking the business. They do not like it. I notice with this man and woman because it seem strange to me."

I was trying to get Maria to remember an actual scene. That's the way the cool detectives do it in the movies.

"What did they have to eat the last time they were in?" The night we were there too. When I waved at them.

"He have the pasta primavera. We do that good, like the old country. She have something plain. Chicken Parmigiana, I think. I remember 'cause I try to get her to have something better. We do everything good. Just some things better. Like I tell you and Karen."

"Did they have wine?"

"Sure. Two bottles. Pinot grigio. The best we got."

"Do you remember what she was wearing?"

Her eyes got a far away look. Then she smiled. "Oh, yes. A pretty yellow dress. Very nice. I think I look good in a dress like that."

"Absolutely." I did my good deed for the day. Maria is a little plump. Pleasantly so I hasten to say.

"You're always bustling about your customers. When you brought their food to the table, Maria, did you hear them mention me or Franklin Farms? Or maybe Guy Mason?" That was the day after Guy Mason died. I was fishing big time here.

She stopped looking at me. At that moment the penny dropped. I could see it in her eyes.

"I do remember something." Her hand went up to her bosom. "I don't know if it's any good. Something they talk about that concern you." She spoke as if she were dredging something deep out of her subconscious.

"Just try to tell me anything you heard. Whatever it is, it will help."

"The beautiful woman. The television star."

"Yellow dress."

She nodded. "I just bring over a new bottle of Pinot Grigio. I opening it so I was standing there. You know how I uncork the wine and pour a little so you can taste it. It take a few minutes."

"Sure."

"They were in a conversation and ignore me standing there."

I tipped my chin slightly to keep her going. My stomach was knotting like a busy boy scout.

"She was in like a business mood, you know, as I say before. So it catch my attention."

"Of course. It would. It seemed funny." I held my breath.

"He say something. How he don't know what you thought

you were doing in the Franklin Farms lawsuit. He use your name. Harris, not Jimmy. He seem angry. I don't know who he is angry with."

Not me, please God.

"And he want to know why she using you for her divorce. She say something about conflict of something. I don't know what. She smile at him and make a big point of it."

Conflict of interest. The thing she waived in writing.

"The man say if that so, they should blow you out of case. She say no, she have better idea, settle with you later, after she control the state. It make no sense to me. How she can control the state, Jimmy? I thought the Governor control the state."

Well, the answer to that one was, "Maybe." But I didn't think Janet was talking politics. I think she said the estate, not the state. This was the day after Guy Mason passed on, remember. Again I marveled at how far Janet Mason was along in her planning.

How she suddenly knew so little about the Franklin Farms lawsuit. And the look on Gino Bartoletti's face in his car when I let it slip Janet was behind it.

This was getting deeper and deeper. I hope I remembered how to paddle a raft of straws.

Chapter 42

On the cab ride back to the office, I let my mind cycle through what Maria had said. I had told the cabby not to rush. He had looked at me like I was out of my mind, which, given the circumstances, wasn't too far off. I sat in the back seat mumbling to myself. I noticed the cabby looking at me in the rear-view mirror. He seemed a tad nervous.

It was pretty clear I had to take whatever steps I could to get out of the Franklin Farms case quickly. I needed to find out how Clyde was making out on publishing notice to Save Our Coast. Damn Susie Wilson for skipping town. She was the only officer. And the only member for all I knew.

I thought maybe I should also hire one of those cheap skip-tracing services to try to find out where she went. That would look good. And I might even be able to get her to sign a dismissal if I could locate her.

But none of that would get me out of the case right away. Not in the day or two I had promised Bartoletti. It was a stupid thing to say. On the other hand, you had to be there.

I thought it might be a good idea to take the publication of service order and my skip-tracer up to Janet Mason and show her that we were trying. Maybe she could keep Gino away. Whatever her relationship was with Gino these days, it was sure as hell a lot better than mine. It was worth a try.

The car behind us honked. The driver shouted something at the cabbie as he roared past. I couldn't make out what he said. It might have helped. I guess we were going too slow. I'd better speed up a lot of things if I hoped to get out of this mess in one piece.

It was dark. We had all the lights on. It's pretty dim in our dining room even then. Karen and I were sitting at the kitchen table. A train rumbled through town. You don't even hear the noise after a while. You just feel it.

Only Bruno looked chipper. He was sitting at the foot of the table looking up at me with beseeching brown eyes. His tail was wagging and his tongue was hanging out. His typical "feed me" pose. I was ignoring him. Bruno doesn't like to be ignored.

Clyde, bless him, had been on top of the service by mail on Save Our Coast. We had the confirmation of our publication orders. We would have to wait for a few weeks for actual publication to be completed so we could file with the court. I had the copies of our confirmation with me.

Finding a cheap skip-tracer had been more difficult than I thought. It had taken me pretty much all afternoon. We finally lined one up and I had the e-mail confirmation of his engagement tucked in my briefcase. Can you believe it, they wanted money in advance? The guy had estimated two weeks to get some results. That's what you get for cheap. But I had a guy. So far, so good.

"I'm going to go up to Franklin Farms tomorrow morning," I said rotating my Hakke Beck on the table. "I'll show Janet what we're doing."

"Do you think it'll do any good?" Karen asked. She put down her glass of wine. I had told Karen about the conversation with Maria. She already knew all about my latest interview with Bartoletti.

"I think so. What more can they ask? I didn't put us in this ridiculous position." Karen was using her finger tip to trace the top of the wineglass. It was round. I could have told her that. She looked up.

"Gino doesn't seem to care a lot about being reasonable." Good point.

"No, but I figure Janet has a lot of reasons to try to calm him down. He didn't seem too happy with her either."

"I guess you're right." Karen sounded weary. Her eyes were starting to droop.

"We should have a bite to eat and get to bed early," I said. I swear to you Bruno understood me. He jumped up and put his front two paws in my lap and started licking my hand. He gave me his "now the guy's talking" look.

Bruno's second and third favorite things are eating and napping. I scratched his ear. You can't quibble with the guy's priorities. "Do you want me to make some pasta or would you prefer an omelet?" I said.

"Whatever you want." She yawned and raised her hand to cover her mouth. "I'm so tired, I think I'll just go to bed." She eats like a mouse.

"Karen?"

She looked up. It must have been my tone. "What?" She opened her eyes.

"Things are so crazy."

"Jimmy, what are you getting at?" Her voice had lost its weariness.

"I mean Guy Mason's death. Bartoletti's threats." I stammered a little. Karen wasn't going to like this. "I'd just feel a lot better if you and Bruno went down to stay with my Mom for a week or two."

"No way." Her eyes sparked. "We're not leaving you here alone. Are you kidding? You're absolutely helpless."

Gosh, that was unfair. Not "absolutely". Come on.

"Besides, Bruno and I are going to help you figure this out. You need us."

"I'm not kidding, Karen. Not this time. There's a thug running around and I don't want you two to be in the wrong place. It's not going to make it any easier for me to have to worry about you."

"We're not going anywhere. I'll worry about me and Bruno. You don't think we'd be worried sick about you if we went to L.A.? No." Her jaw was set. You don't live with a woman for eight years without recognizing her moods. When Karen gets her mind made up, she's stubborn. I'm tenacious. She's just stubborn.

"Okay, just promise me if things start going bad you'll reconsider."

She reached over and put her hand on my arm. A little affectionate smile trickled across her lips. Her look softened. I think I saw tears. Then she leaned over the table and kissed me.

She hadn't answered me.

Chapter 43

"Janet." I waited.

"Janet," I called out again.

She hadn't answered the phone. I didn't want to embarrass her. Normally I wouldn't have come until I'd gotten hold of her. But I was antsy and it was worth a drive up to Franklin Farms.

It was a pretty cool day and there was a breeze. Not pool weather. But Janet hadn't answered the doorbell so I was poking my nose gingerly around the side of the house. I didn't want to catch her skinny-dipping. At least, not a lot.

I was wearing my court outfit. Sports coat, dark slacks, blue button-down shirt and one of my three ties. I was carrying my battered leather briefcase.

"Janet," I called out again as I turned the corner of the house.

Janet was floating face down in the pool, naked. She was utterly still. I froze. Then I realized she might still be alive. I dropped my briefcase and ran as fast as I could across the lawn. Janet's blue baseball cap was upside down on the apron of the pool. I kicked it aside as I ran past and shrugged off my sports coat.

The dive I executed, shoes and all, was not the picture of Olympic perfection but I took three strokes and grabbed her. I paddled over to the side. I tried to get her out of the pool but I couldn't lift her. No leverage. I didn't think she was breathing.

I grabbed her under the arm and held her head up. With the other hand, I worked my way along the side of the pool to the shallow end. I went up the steps backwards, water streaming from my slacks and shoes and pulled her out behind me. It's incredible how much an unconscious person weighs. I stepped on my jacket and almost tripped.

"Damn it, what was that CPR technique they taught me in high school." I said that to an empty lawn. I got Janet on to her back with her head to one side. There was a bruise on the side of her face. I opened her mouth and cleared her tongue. Then I breathed into her mouth. I rocked back on my heels, pushed on her chest and counted. "One, two three, four," I called aloud. My voice had an odd, hysterical quality.

Then I breathed into her mouth again. It didn't seem to be doing any good. She looked waxy. I did it again and again. Then I turned her over and tried pressing on her back to get her to start breathing. I'm sure I made a mess of it.

It didn't matter. She was dead.

I sat beside her for the longest time. Maybe I was in shock. I kept staring at that blue baseball cap, the red letters saying, "Desperate Shop Girls". The sunlight glinted off her six carat diamond ring. The only sound was the pool filter working at the glittering water. I might be sitting there now if I hadn't started shivering in the cool breeze.

I got onto my knees and then I threw up on the lawn. I'd never seen a dead body before. I mean I've seen a dead body. I saw my Uncle Jerry in the funeral home. But I'd never seen a live dead body, if you follow.

I wiped my mouth with the back of my hand. I crawled away and struggled to my feet. I was a sight. Soaking wet, grass stains on my knees.

My teeth were chattering. I needed to get warm. I also had to get to a telephone. I walked unsteadily towards the house.

The sliding doors to the back of the house were unlocked. "Anyone here?" My voice shook. The house was cold. No heat. No lights. No answer.

I squelched across the wood floor in the den leaving puddles in my wake, turning on lights as I went. Through the living room. I turned right. It looked like the bedrooms were that way. I checked the doors in the hallway to see if I could find a linen closet. None.

I opened the door to a bedroom. I stripped the blanket off the bed and shed my clothes. I sat on the edge of the bed and wrapped myself in the blanket until my teeth stopped chattering. That's when I noticed the phone on the table. I picked it up and dialed 911. Then I went back into the living room and lit a fire in the gas fireplace.

That's where I was, naked and wrapped in a blanket when Chief Carsone showed up. He hunkered down next to the chair I'd pulled up to the fireplace. "Howdy, Mr. Harris." He slowly masticated the wad of gum in his mouth.

I looked over at him and nodded. I was still too cold to speak. Maybe I was still in shock too, I don't know.

He pushed back his hat and its badge caught the firelight. "You sure seem to get in a lot of trouble these days. Why do you think that is now?"

I was hoping he would tell me. "Are you investigating the accident, Chief?"

"Nope. County sheriff. Not sure it's an accident, are we?"

251

Weren't we?

"Sheriff's department's on its way up. They'll be here in two shakes of a lamb's tail."

"Didn't you investigate the Guy Mason accident?"

"Nope. Helped the sheriff out is all." He snapped his gum.

"Why are you here?"

"Oh, heard the call on the police radio. Thought I might come up here and keep you company."

Great. "Can I make a call? I need to let my wife know I'll be late so she won't worry." Wife? I also needed a change of clothes. I was getting a little self-conscious.

He shook his head and popped his gum again. "Can't disturb a crime scene."

I pointed out to him I'd already used the phone to call 911. I admit I was a little testy. I get that way when I discover a dead body.

"No harm then, I suppose. Already wiped out any evidence." That made me feel a lot better.

Two hours later I had answered all the questions a deputy sheriff had posed to me at least three different times. He was a nice young man with short brown hair and a kind smile. He spoke in a quiet, soothing voice. The pleats in his light brown shirt were as sharp as a razor. I didn't trust him. I've seen too many "Columbo"s.

Policemen were crawling all over the place, taking pictures and examining the house. The Coroner had been and gone. Janet had been taken away, zipped in a bag. That shook me more than anything.

At least I'd been able to change into the jeans and a flannel shirt Clyde had brought up to the house. A deputy went to the door to get the clothes. I can tell you, it's pretty intimidating to answer a police officer's questions when you're huddled, bare-ass naked in a blanket. I was so scared, I even told them about Gino Bartoletti. Call me dumb.

The police wouldn't let Clyde or Karen in. They'd gone back down to the office to wait. That had been about an hour ago.

It was 2 o'clock. I hadn't had any lunch. And I had tossed up breakfast on the lawn. I was ravenous all of a sudden. Before I could ask for a sandwich or something, the deputy folded up his pad and got up.

"Guess you can go now, Mr. Harris. We'll call you if we need you. Not going any place are you?"

"I'll be around. What do you think happened?"

"Don't know yet. Could have been an accident. Seems a little cold to go swimming naked like that though."

"Do you have any idea when it happened?"

"Coroner says maybe last night." When Karen and I were talking about my bringing over the stuff we were working on. We might have been saying her name as she drowned.

"Well, thanks," I said. I got up too, with a groan. I was stiff and sore. I felt like I'd been run over by a gray Mercedes.

Then I shivered.

Chapter 44

"You look terrible," Karen said. She put her arm around me and guided me to a chair in her office. She took a Diet Coke out of the little refrigerator and put it down in front of me.

"You do look like shit," Clyde added. Clyde likes to comfort me. Bruno was lying beside Karen's desk. He didn't venture an opinion.

They were right. I picked up the Diet Coke and took a sip. It was 3 o'clock. Lunch hadn't helped much. I felt empty. I'd come back to the office because I knew Karen and Clyde were waiting for me.

"Thank, heaps," I said. I tried to smile. I don't know if I made it. "I'm all right."

That was a whopper. I was exhausted and I was scared. If Janet Mason's death wasn't an accident, we were in terrible trouble. And two accidental deaths in a matter of weeks was starting to stretch the limits of my optimistic nature.

As calmly as I could, I told them what had happened at

Franklin Farms. I tried to answer their questions, leaving out the graphic details.

Karen looked worried. She leaned forward and put her hand on my arm. She was looking at me closely with those big green eyes. I was doing my best to avoid them.

"Maybe you should go home," she said.

I was drooping. "No, I don't want to be alone right now."

"I could come with you."

The truth was, I had to think. And I didn't want to do it at home. I needed to be alone with people. Not together.

"You're busy," I said. I gestured towards the pile of papers on her desk. "Let's stay here a while. Maybe it'll help if I do some work."

I got up slowly and I made it into my office, closing the door behind me. I nearly bumped Bruno in the nose, poor guy. He sounded hurt when I didn't let him come in.

I collapsed into my desk chair. I stared at my binoculars for a while. I closed my eyes. That didn't do any good. My mind refused to engage.

My eyes fixed on a bottle of Dom Perignon we had left in the corner of my office when we took the box home. A future celebration. I had forgotten it was there. I couldn't take my eyes off it.

I went over and picked it up and set it in the center of my desk. I sat staring at it. I needed a drink. How was I going to get out of this? How could I protect Karen?

There had been two deaths. And one disappearance. We still didn't know where Susie Wilson was or if she was okay. God.

No sounds. It was just me and that bottle. I rubbed at my eye with my hand. It was still tender. I picked the bottle up and turned it around, looking at the liquid inside. I changed my grip. I reached up and twisted out the cork. It popped. Warm champagne fizzed over my hand and dripped on my jeans. I didn't care. The smell filled the room. I was scared out of my wits. I set the bottle back down on the desk.

I stared at the bottle some more. I couldn't hold my shoulders up I felt so tired. I reached towards the bottle. Then I drew my hand back. I knew if I went down that road, I'd be in trouble. We all would. But I needed it. I started to reach for the bottle again.

Then in an act of anger that took me by surprise, I shifted my grasp and gripped the long neck of the bottle. With a single motion, I turned in my chair and heaved it as hard as I could against the wall. Unfortunately I have lousy aim. I was never much good at baseball.

The bottle went straight through the window. Much to my regret, I hadn't opened it when I came into my office. The window shattered with a deafening crash. I cringed down in my chair.

The door burst open. Karen and Clyde jostled each other through the doorway. I focused on Karen's face. Her eyes were wide open in fear. Bruno trundled in a couple of moments later. He was good at not getting underfoot. That is a terrific idea when you're built as low to the ground as Bruno is. He's learned the hard way.

Bruno's head moved right and left sniffing the air. I was wiping my hands back and forth on the legs of my jeans. He looked at me inquiringly and padded over to sniff at my pants.

"Jimmy, what happened?" Karen said. "Was it another gunshot? "Are you okay?" Her voice was half an octave above normal.

Clyde had gone over to the side of the window and was peering cautiously around the edge.

"No. It was my fault," I said to Karen. "Nothing to worry about."

"What's that smell?" Karen said.

"What smell?" I hoped my face was as innocent as my voice. Bruno sat down in front of me and started wagging his tail. I eyeballed him. My eyes said "No, Bruno. Go away." Bruno wasn't listening to my eyeballs. He sat there on his haunches, looking up at me expectantly.

"What happened?" Karen asked, the fear still in her face.

Clyde looked over at me. He had seen the champagne bottle, judging by his look. Keep your mouth shut, my mind screamed. I got up and put my arm around Karen. I turned her and walked with her towards the door.

"I guess I was more uptight than I thought. I picked something up and threw it out the window. I'm sorry."

Karen started crying. I guess this was getting to her too. Why not? She leaned into me like she didn't have the energy to walk anymore.

"I think you were right," I said. We should go home."

I turned back to Clyde and mouthed "Thank You." He nodded and smiled. He raised his fist and pumped it sharply down towards his body with a nod. Then he winked at me. I smiled back at him.

I said to Clyde, "Maybe you should have Pamela call that glass guy and see if he can fix the window again." Support your local business, I always say.

Bruno looked uncertain as Karen and I started to leave. He gave a small bark and waddled after us. We had forgotten him. Wow. We had forgotten Bruno. He wouldn't put up with it. I looked back. "Come on, boy," I said. "We're going home." One big, happy family.

I realized I felt better. At least about myself.

Chapter 45

"Stand still," Karen said. I was shifting from foot to foot and wiggling around.

We were up bright and early. I had fallen into a dreamless sleep last night. A full eight hours. I felt more like myself. Which isn't necessarily good. Judging from Karen's face, she'd slept well too. She looked rested.

"I can't," I said. "You're tickling me." She had a tape measure pushed into the crotch of my boxer shorts. We were standing in the living room near the window. Any of our curious neighbors were getting their morning's entertainment.

"If you want a new pair of slacks, I have to get you're inseam." She pulled the tape measure taunt between my crotch and just above the inside of my ankle. She let go of one end of the tape measure and noted the measurement down on a form with the stub of a pencil she took from behind her ear.

"Are you sure the coat and slacks will be ready next Thursday," I asked. "I have to be in court on our motion for a writ of attachment against Clarence. You know, so we can collect the sanctions he owes us."

The sound of Bruno's soft snoring was the musical accompaniment to our tailoring session. He was still asleep on the end of our bed. The door was open and I could see his brown fur rising and falling.

"All I can tell you is Lands' End said if we order the clothes today and have them shipped out by expedited delivery, they'll be here next Wednesday."

Karen was kneeling down in front of me with the tape measure. The neckline of her blouse had fallen forward as she leaned over. She doesn't wear a bra.

The tickle in my crotch changed to a more pleasurable feeling. I reached down and slipped my hand into her blouse. She batted it away and shook her head. It made her breasts jiggle. She didn't even look up.

"Stop that if you don't want to go to court buck naked." She stood up, turned aside and flipped over to the back of the order form. Her finger found the place she wanted and she started reading the instructions for another measurement. The tiny red tip of her tongue poked out between her teeth. She's real cute when she concentrates on something.

My little manly friend slipped its head out of my boxer shorts. He gets curious at the most unexpected moments. Karen was occupied with her measurements.

"Let's see," she said, turning back. "Point of shoulder to just above the top of the hand. Okay." She put the tape measure against my arm and penciled another number. She has great focus. Then again, so do I.

I leaned over and nuzzled her neck. Then I touched my tongue to the place in her neck where her pulse beats. "You taste good."

She sighed. I poked up against her.

She slapped at me playfully and looked up into my baby blue eyes. "Out with it now," she said. "Are you trying to get something straight between us?"

"Absolutely."

She peered down and brought her hand to her lips with a little gasp. "Oh my. Good morning," she said to my little friend. My friend is her friend too. "Look who's poking around."

She reached down and took me in her hand. I felt a warm surge well up through my body, like I always do. Then she leaned forward and kissed me on the lips. A very lustful kiss, if I do say so myself. The woman is easily aroused. Thank goodness.

"I guess I'm going to have to take care of him," she nodded down towards our friend, "if we're going to get anything done here." She draped the tape measure around her neck and sank to her knees. The lucky stiff. I put my hands gently on top of her soft hair and watched the pencil behind her ear start to doodle in the air.

I don't remember much after that. Nothing that I'd care to relate. You'll have to ask the neighbors. We forgot to pull down the window shades. I'm pretty sure they couldn't see in anyway.

It must have been an hour later before we got all my measurements down. Time well spent, I'd say. Bruno was still snoring away. That dog can sleep through anything.

"Okay, I think that's it," Karen said. She made a final notation and tapped the tip of the pencil once against the order form. "I'll call Lands' End and order the clothes. Are you sure you like the blue blazer and gray slacks?" I needed a new sports coat. I'd left the old one at Janet's. It had disappeared.

"I think they'll look good. Don't you?"

"I'll be proud to be seen with you. I think we should get you a couple of new ties."

I nodded my head eagerly. I was in a mellow mood.

"I'll take care of it," she said. She pulled out the drawer and dropped the tape measure back in.

Uh, Karen." She looked up over the edge of her coffee cup. I brew a mean pot of coffee. Bruno raised his muzzle up off his paws and started wagging his tail. He'd decided to join us in the kitchen. I think he thought we might feed him again. Bruno has great concentration as well.

"Janet Mason," I said.

She put down the cup. "What about her?" Karen was intently focused on me now.

"You know, if it wasn't an accident, I may have gotten her killed." My finger traced a circle on the table.

"Jimmy, sometimes you're an idiot." She didn't say it unkindly but her lips went hard.

"I know, but I was the one that told Gino Bartoletti about the Franklin Farms lawsuit."

"You can't blame yourself for that. It was the truth. You didn't know anything would happen."

"You're right," I conceded. "But we still could be in serious trouble." I stopped and looked at her pretty face. "Are you sure you won't go down to LA. Please. I really want you to."

She didn't say anything. She just watched my eyes.

"You know I'll miss you. But I'll feel a lot better if you were down with my Mom."

Her jaw firmed. "Jimmy, we've been through this before. Bruno and I are not leaving. We'd be worried sick about you."

She reached over and put her hand on my forearm. This is one stubborn woman. I love her that way, but it didn't make me feel any better.

Chapter 46

"I heard about Janet Mason." I was sitting in my office with the telephone in my hand. Special Agent Leary's cheery voice was not exactly what I wanted to hear so early in the morning. "Too bad," he said. He didn't exactly seem broken up about it.

"Do you think it was an accident?" I couldn't help myself. I had to ask.

"I don't know. It's not my concern. I was hoping to chat with her again." He made it sound like she ruined his day, floating around like that.

"You chatted with her before?"

"Sure. After you and I had our talk."

"Why are you telling me this?"

"No reason. I just wanted to mention she seemed upset to see me. Any idea why?"

I may be dumb but I'm not stupid. Neither is Special Agent Leary. I let the silence seep down the line.

"Maybe you made her nervous?" I said finally. He certainly made me nervous.

"Maybe. If you think of anything, give me a call."

"Right away." I started to hang up when I heard an echo of his voice. I put the phone back to my ear. "Sorry, I didn't hear that. Say again."

"I thought you might like to know that Gino Bartoletti has been indicted for looting the United Union Pension Fund and for tax evasion."

"Really. Well, that makes me feel better. He's in jail?"

Leary laughed unpleasantly. "Oh, sure. For about 20 minutes before he made bail."

I suddenly had an urge to go. "Ah. Well, goodbye. I'll call if I think of something."

I believe Special Agent Leary was trying to scare me. Now that I was his best remaining source for information on Gino Bartoletti's involvement in Franklin Farms. Of course, you can't scare a man like me. And as soon as I change my pants, I'm going to talk to Karen about taking our friend's cottage in Morro Bay for the next couple of weeks.

This wasn't good. We still weren't out of the Franklin Farms case. I was standing between Bartoletti and a clean sale of Franklin Farms, assuming his foreclosure was signed off before Janet's unfortunate demise. And I'll bet it was. Potentially I was also his ticket to jail. I pulled at my collar. It was getting hot in here.

"Clyde," I yelled. I really need to learn how to use the intercom system one of these days.

We were still nowhere on locating Susie Wilson. The skip-tracer was giving us our money's worth. And our publication of notice to Save Our Coast had two weeks to run.

I was jumpy as we drove home. Karen and I had been out pretty late. It was too dark and too lonely. Besides, I was making Bruno nervous. I let him out of the car first. I figured he'd make the smallest target. He shuffled off towards the front door without a whimper. I took that for a good sign. I put my arm around Karen and hurried her to the door.

I stepped on an envelope as I opened it. I reached down and tore open the flap. There was a scrap of paper inside. I unfolded it. Too dark to see. I reached over and flipped on the light switch.

The note was straight-forward enough. "Get out. Now!" Typed on cheap paper. No signature. Nothing. I took it as a hint. I passed it over to Karen.

It was time to leave. At least to get far enough away to make us invisible. This time Karen agreed with me wholeheartedly. I'd sing her praises to you, but I've got a lousy voice. Ask anyone.

We bundled Bruno and a couple of suitcases into the Jag and split. I couldn't go too far. I had a court date next Thursday and I needed to have access to my office. In the dead of night, if necessary.

Our friend's cottage is a small old house right on the beach just beyond the rock in Morro Bay. Even though it's smaller than our place, we made ourselves cozy. Bruno liked running out the front door onto the sand.

Our first week there was just about everything we had hoped. Which means nothing. We got to feeling almost normal again. Neither of us had set foot in San Buenasera.

I figured we were doing okay. It was Wednesday. The only thing was, I had to go back to our house in San Buenasera tonight to pick up the package of clothes from Lands' End so I'd have something to wear to court tomorrow. I set out at midnight.

I switched off my headlights as I turned onto our street. I didn't see any strange cars. It's a little hard to tell, what with all the comings and goings. There are a lot of single people in our neighborhood. You know how it is. Besides, there are a lot of little side streets.

I left the headlights off and rolled to a stop at the curb in front of our house. The dome light in the car lit me up as I opened the door. So much for my skills at espionage. I slammed the car door and darted for the porch, keeping low. Hot damn, there was the package.

I grabbed it and ran back to the car. Then I high-tailed it out of town. I didn't notice the gray Mercedes that rolled out behind me. I ask you, how could I? He didn't have his lights on.

"All rise." Judge Sandra Anderson entered the courtroom in her black silk robes. Swish. She sat down behind the bench. Swish. We sat. Bang. She called the court to order.

"Good morning, Mr. Harris." She looked over at me and smiled. I think it was the new threads. I did look really spiffy.

Then she turned to Clarence Jenkins' counsel. "Mr. Pommeset." She nodded towards him. She wasn't smiling anymore. I thought old Pommeset was going to expire right there. Judge Anderson looked down and shuffled through some papers in front of her.

"Mr. Pommeset," she said, looking up. "I'm inclined to grant this writ of attachment. Mr. Jenkins is testing my patience." She pointed her gavel at him. "Can you tell me why he hasn't paid Mr. Harris the sanctions I ordered? And why I have to spend more of the court's time on this matter?"

Pommeset rose unevenly to his feet. Pommeset is way too old and fat to be called a lamb, but he certainly looked like he was being led to slaughter. He cleared his throat.

"Your honor. My client is in financial distress. His business has been impacted." I know that's a lie. I'd been supplying him business lately at a rapid clip.

"What proof do you have to provide the court, Mr. Pommeset?"

"Your honor . . ."

"The proof, Mr. Pommeset."

"But . . ."

"No 'buts', Mr. Pommeset, if you don't have proof to present to this court, I'm going to grant the writ."

Now, Judge Anderson was being unfair to old Andrew Pommeset, as I'm about to explain. I'm not complaining, you understand. She was probably overcome by my nifty blue blazer and gray slacks. Maybe she saw me as a husband number four. That wouldn't work. Karen could take her.

It's one of the oldest adages at the bar and dear to all trial lawyers. If the facts are on your side, argue the facts. If the law's on your side, argue the law. If neither is on your side, argue like hell.

Bang. We got our writ.

I was so pleased I didn't notice the hearse following me home a few cars back. Call me unobservant.

Chapter 47

It was around dawn, in the moments between sleep and wakefulness. The crash of the surf provided a comforting rhythm of sound. The gunshot tore apart the wisps of a pleasant little sex dream.

I rolled over and looked into Karen's wide-open eyes. As always, I knew exactly what to say. "Oh, shit." I'm so succinct.

Well, one good thing, this had happened to us so often we didn't drop to the floor and cover our heads. Even Bruno wasn't cringing under the bed. I think we felt more resignation than fear. I know I did. Not that we weren't cautious.

We got up and threw on the essentials. It was cold and a little blowy outside. I shivered in the breeze. At least I think there was the breeze. A couple of neighbors had their lights on. A few people had stepped out onto their front lawns peering curiously towards our cottage. Not many. A lot of the cottages were weekend homes or rentals and this wasn't exactly high season. All in all, it was pretty deserted.

We made straight for the Jaguar. There she was, lying dead, the noble beast. A bullet in her engine. Her sleek lines slumbered now. Her growl was stilled. My heart broke. Hey, I'm a sentimental guy.

Karen and I joined hands. I needed to make her feel better. She loved the Jaguar too. I adopted my best television announcer's voice. I sounded pretty good, I thought.

"Honey, don't cry," I said. She wasn't crying, but there's no harm in saying that. "We have the technology, We have the capability. We can fix her. Even better than she was before." Was Karen old enough to remember the "Six Million Dollar Man"? I just hoped it wouldn't cost $6 million. Forget inflation. "She'll run again." How I do go on.

Karen looked up. Her lips cut a thin, straight line across her face. "Can the stupid humor. You can be an idiot sometimes." She said it with deep admiration. You simply have to be able to read between the lines, like I can. "Clarence Jenkins?" she asked.

"Looks like it." I was going to have to do something about that guy. Something drastic. I just needed to figure out what. A gust of wind caromed across the sand. I turned aside.

"Are you going to call the police?"

"Yeah. And AAA. Oh, and State Farm. Our good neighbor will surely want to know about this." One thing, I had the drill down pat.

"I'll put in a call to Mike too as soon as he opens." I sighed. "I'd better find out how much a new engine's going to cost. Maybe he can get a used one cheap." I figured old Jaguars were dropping dead right and left. There had to be one that had died with a good engine. "He needs to check out the car too. The brakes are a little soft. I noticed it on the way back from court yesterday." Apparently when I should have been looking in my rear view mirror.

The AAA guy had the car lifted onto the flatbed of his tow truck. "Tow her to Mike's Garage," I said. I didn't really have to tell the AAA driver. We'd been through this before. He nodded and handed me the clipboard to sign and climbed back into his truck.

Karen and I were alone. Everyone else was long gone. The sun had burned through the mist. I had my arm around her as we watched the Jaguar disappear around the corner, perched precariously on the back of the tow truck, trying to look sleek but hunched down and clinging to the truck for dear life. Karen looked up at me.

"What should we do now?"

"I think we should go to a hotel in San Luis. I'd feel better."

"So would I," she said.

And we did, although we had to reason it out with Bruno. He likes the beach.

"You're the luckiest son of a bitch in Christendom," Mike said.

Well, yeah. But Mike doesn't know Karen all that well. So I figured he had something else in mind. Maybe about the car. Astounding mental perspicacity. It's the legal training.

It was four days later. In the morning. Mike was calling me at the hotel with an update, like I'd asked him to. The hotel we'd checked into was one of the small ones, over near the Mission. Convenient, but not a tourist place. Besides they took pets. It cost me $4 extra per day for Bruno. I intend to deduct it from his allowance.

"Yeah. But exactly why?" I said.

"I got the engine in. I picked one up for 1400 bucks and it cost about $600 in labor."

"That's good. But it can't be why I'm the luckiest guy in Christendom."

"No. Not that. I'm checking the car over like you told me."

"Uh huh." I shifted the phone to the other hand and changed positions. My pants were cutting into my crotch. I pulled at them. "So?"

"You had a leak in the brake fluid line. There was a hole in it. The fluid was bone dry. I checked the hand brake and the cable was almost frayed through. The fuel line was leaking too."

This was not good.

"With the fuel line in the engine leaking like it was, I'm surprised the car didn't blow up when the engine was shot. If you'd hit something, it wouldn't have been pretty."

Gino had found us. Damn. And my old buddy Clarence Jenkins had saved our lives. He had shot the Jaguar dead. Before it killed me. Go figure.

Now I knew what I was going to do to him. Something dramatic. I was going to find the little rabbit and give him a big kiss on the lips. That ought to confuse him.

And I also knew what to do next.

"Special Agent Leary?"

"Speaking."

"This is James Harris, the attorney from San Buenasera. Do you remember you told me to call you."

"I do."

"Gino Bartoletti made an attempt on my life." I said it with just a tad less drama than "They're hitting the beach at Normandy".

"I'm sorry to hear that, Mr. Harris." He didn't sound too bothered.

"Shouldn't we talk or something." I was looking out the second story window at the hotel parking lot, scanning the area for lurking felons.

"I don't know if that's necessary, Mr. Harris."

"I mean if I co-operate, won't you give me, like protection?"

"Why should we do that?"

My scrotum did its tightening thing. "To protect me and my family! So I can help you," I added cunningly.

"I don't see how you can help us, Mr. Harris. Maybe you should report this to your local police."

"But you were so anxious to talk to me."

"That was before we picked up Carlo Peso.

I chewed on that name. "Who?" Mr. Leary was getting on my nerves.

"Gino Bartoletti's muscle.

"Broad shouldered guy, no neck, bald?"

"That's him. Looks like a fireplug. Mr. Peso's seen the light. He's agreed to turn state's evidence. He's singing like a canary."

"Singing like a canary?" The guy was giddy.

"I've always wanted to say that." He gave a small chuckle. I didn't know the FBI permitted that.

"Is that good?"

"What? Singing like a canary?"

"No. What Peso is telling you."

"Good enough for us to pick up Gino Bartoletti. I don't think his lawyer's going to have such an easy time getting him out."

"Are you sure?"

"Well, Mr. Harris, we've implicated Mr. Bartoletti in several killings including Janet Mason's."

"Peso told you that?"

"Sure, why not? We gave him immunity."

"You're kidding. You gave immunity to a killer."

"People die all the time, Mr. Harris. We have bigger concerns."

"You've got to be kidding."

"I'm not. We'll give Gino Bartoletti immunity too in return for the right information. He has some friends we'd like to chat with." Our Federal government in action. They'd just put me in jail and throw away the key. "And put him in a witness protection program to boot. He could be your new neighbor." FBI humor.

"So I guess you really don't need me." I may have sounded a tad depressed.

"No." Leary let down a little. "I wouldn't be too worried anyway. I don't think there's any danger to you or your family. We think Bartoletti probably doesn't have anything more to gain by eliminating you." I wanted to know the exact odds that went into "probably". "And you can't give us any information we don't have" he continued. "Not that you could have in the first place."

Ingrate. I, however, held my tongue. I have no idea whether these FBI guys have drinks with my friends at the IRS. Better to play it safe.

"Thanks. Let me know if you need me." What I meant is, I hope I never hear from you again. But I think Special Agent Leary knew that. I started to replace the phone on the cradle.

"Mr. Harris." His voice sounded different. Not so aloof. I put the phone back in my ear. He had my attention.

"Yes."

He cleared his throat. There was a moment of silence before he spoke. "I have to be in Santa Barbara next week. I think you might find it useful to meet me there."

Now what?

"Karen, you're never going to believe this . . ." I told her everything. "I think we can go home now." I grabbed my suitcase down from the rack. "Get Bruno."

Chapter 48

Stearns Wharf in Santa Barbara grasps out at the water with an open hand. It has a magical quality in the sunlight of early spring, a celebrity, surrounded by the popping flashbulbs of sun bounding off the clamoring waves.

Special Agent Leary and I strolled by the new Sea Center, heading out towards Moby Dick's and the ocean beyond. Leary still looked like Dick Tracy. He was dressed in a dark blue suit and a red tie. No tan rain coat. I'm sure he would have been mistaken for a tourist if the people we passed hadn't been forced to raise their hands to their eyes in panic, blinded by the reflection off his black shoes.

I, on the other hand, looked really cool in my pressed jeans and new gray turtleneck cashmere sweater with the sleeves pushed up on my arms. I have great forearms. They're the second strongest part of my body. My matching Nikes were being universally admired. I had taken the precaution of wearing sunglasses, so I could look directly at Leary without blinking.

"You caused me a lot of trouble," Leary said. He had a gruff voice.

"Gosh, I'm sorry. Why?" I meant that honestly, no matter how it sounded. I'm a boy scout at heart.

"You're so dumb is why. You nearly got yourself killed."

My Nike caught in one of the heavy, uneven planks of the wharf. Leary put a steadying hand on my arm.

"Clumsy too," he said.

This did not sit well with me. The "got yourself killed" part, I mean. Dumb, I admit to. That's why I had accepted Special Agent Leary's invitation and driven down to Santa Barbara. I was hoping he would shed some light on the dim recesses of my mind. I mean I would have come anyway. You don't fool around with the FBI, but I had ulterior motives. Or were they interior motives?

"You frighten me," I said.

"That's the first intelligent thing I've heard you say."

He fell silent and gazed out over the water. A pelican, it's huge yellow beak supporting the pouch hanging below, seemed to occupy his attention. He pointed to the bird. "They always remind me of pterodactyls," he said.

I waited a good 10 seconds. Then I couldn't stand it anymore. "Are you going to tell me how?"

"How what?"

"How I almost got myself killed."

"I was hoping you'd ask." He offered me a bleak smile that did nothing to make me feel better. "We were tapping Janet Mason's phone. This was a few days before she died. She was pushing Bartoletti to kill you. You were very lucky. He wanted you to clean up the Franklin Farms lawsuit first."

"Why didn't you call the police and tell them?" For goodness sake, I could have been killed.

"Come on. You know I couldn't compromise our investigation. We'd been working to get Gino Bartoletti for three years." He gestured and we continued walking down the pier.

"So you'd just let him kill me?"

"I called you. You remember that? I was trying to scare you. I hoped you'd take the hint." He turned his head and looked at me. He shook his head. "You didn't."

"I thought you were trying to get me to testify," I said. "But how could you just leave me twisting in the wind?"

"That's the problem. I couldn't. I must be getting soft. So I had the note put under your door."

"What note?"

"You know. 'Get out. Now!'"

"You sent that? You scared the hell out of me and my wife." There it was again, "wife".

"You don't sound very grateful."

"Couldn't you just have called me and told me? Not that subtle stuff."

"And take the chance you'd tell someone. No way. Besides, I didn't think what I said was so subtle. You can be pretty thick when you want to."

"What about Janet Mason?"

"I told you, we got a confession from Carlo Peso."

"I mean, did you let him kill her."

"We didn't have that choice. We didn't know you'd spilled the beans to Gino."

Spilled the beans? How could he know I had told Gino about Janet being behind the Franklin Farms lawsuit?

I came to an abrupt stop. Leary took two more steps before he turned and came back to me. "What do you mean?"

"Come on, we do talk to the police, Mr. Harris. At least, they talk to us."

"I see. Well yeah, I feel terrible about that slip. I didn't do it on purpose." At least, I don't think I did. There was a lurking doubt somewhere deep down inside. "It's been bothering me."

"Don't let it. Janet Mason played everyone she was involved with. Gino, you. Susie Wilson. Even her husband. We searched her papers after she died. The way we put it together, she had her husband killed."

We paused as a father with four small children in tow passed us. Kids were running this way and that and the daddy was shouting. They weren't paying any attention. A woman was following a few steps behind with all the accoutrements of a vacation, a towel, suntan oil, a paperback book. She had this weird expression on her face, as if she was enjoying the spectacle in a perverse kind of way. Maybe she was just shell-shocked.

Leary watched them pass, then shook his head. "You have any kids?"

"No." I wasn't about to try to explain my marital status. I couldn't do that, even to myself. So I changed the subject. "How'd Janet manage that?"

"What?"

"Having Guy Mason killed."

"Oh. She promised Franklin Farms to Bartollti. Free and clear. Everything ready to build. Fully entitled. He'd invested everything he had in it. Everything he'd looted from the pension fund. More importantly, a huge hunk of his employer's money." Leary turned and walked over to the edge of the pier. I followed. I was a Scout once, so I'm hard to lose. He put both hands on the railing and stared out.

"The pension fund?" I said. Leary turned and gave me a look. He pursed his mouth and shook his head in disgust. I may have been wrong.

"No, Mr. Harris. Not the pension fund. Gambrella family money." Leary put his finger against the side of his nose. "Family money, as in mob money. This was going to be his big score. Only the family didn't know he was participating. They wouldn't have approved. But it looked like a sure thing." He turned back and looked out to the water as he spoke. A sailboat sent its bow into an errant wave. "Acreage, ocean views. Enormous demand. And a way for the Gambrella family to launder huge drug profits."

"If he'd built it, he'd have made a fortune, even if he had to share with Guy Mason." I sounded like I knew what I was talking about.

"Maybe. That's certainly what Guy Mason wanted to do. It's the only way Mason made any real money. But it would have taken years. Bartoletti had it arranged so he was the financier. Way behind the scenes, along with his friends, but with most of the profits from the development coming to them. That's where you came in. At least from Janet's point of view.

"Huh?" I shuffled my feet.

"Your job originally was to put pressure on Bartoletti by delaying the project until Janet could figure out a way to get Bartoletti to take care of her husband. When we raided the pension plan everything changed." He paused. "Let's walk." He made a gesture towards the end of the pier. He seemed to drift off into thought.

"So," I finally said.

"Oh. We accidentally helped Janet out. Gino came under enormous pressure from his friends. And remember, he hadn't told them about his investment. He needed out quickly. His friends didn't like the idea of being associated with the project anymore. That's why he became, shall we say, overexcited."

"Janet was in his way."

"He was furious when he found out she was using him. Gino Bartoletti is a very dangerous man. He was a nasty fellow before he became an executive. Your Janet Mason was riding the tiger. She just was blind to how big and bad the tiger really was."

"So I became the problem."

"Yes, you did. With the rights to build that your City Council granted, he could have flipped the property and still made a fortune."

"But I had it stopped cold before Janet died," I said, thinking it through. "Why wasn't he concerned then?"

"He was. But Janet held him back. She told him someone else would just bring the lawsuit. You got lucky. Guy Mason shrugged you off as just a normal problem he'd work out in due course. He cooled Bartoletti down. As time dragged on, Janet poisoned the well and convinced Bartoletti that her husband was screwing him over. Trying to get a better deal for himself."

"Janet wasn't a nice person."

"You might say that." His voice was heavy with sarcasm. "But, you messed her up. We heard her screaming about you over the telephone. What did you do?"

Leary and I steered our way around an ice cream cone that some kid had dropped. A seagull was picking at it while another seagull protested. I think I'd seen the gull in court last week. I don't soar with eagles.

"You're not going to believe this," I said. I didn't believe it either. "I was being ethical. I wouldn't drop the Franklin

Farms suit because of Susie Wilson and SOC. They were my clients, not Janet."

"Who's SOC."

"A little charitable organization that fights for the coastline. Very, very little as it turns out."

Leary grunted.

"Do you know what happened to Susie Wilson?"

"Yeah, Leary said, turning to look at me. "We traced her to a small town in Northern California. Called Ferndale, I think. She's working part-time at a hair salon and interning at some classic rock radio station up there. Hippie kind of place."

"She'd enjoy that. I'm glad she's okay. She was a little dippy, but I liked her."

"Janet scared her off after she got her to sign some papers."

"The release we got in the mail."

"Yeah, I suppose. But Wilson was lucky. Janet couldn't get Bartoletti involved. She was scared Wilson might blab something about her. If he had been involved, I'm pretty sure she wouldn't be up in Ferndale now. Maybe under it."

"But then why did she sic Gino on me?"

"No choice. He was the only one left who could deal with you. Besides, she thought you were an idiot."

"Thanks."

"He gave me his FBI smile. "You're welcome.""

"Can I ask you a question?" We'd reached the end of the wharf. We'd have been looking at China except this big island was in the way. An old guy was fishing on our right. His rod was leaning against the railing. He was sitting on a little stool with his eyes closed and his hands folded in his lap. There were no fish in his bucket. He had this serene look on his face. I think he and Bruno are related.

"Sure."

I closed my eyes and let the breeze blow over me for a moment or two. Then I looked at Leary. "Why are you telling me all this? Aren't FBI agents supposed to be tight-lipped and all that."

"Well, yeah, we are. But the case is closed now and we have Bartoletti in jail. There's no harm in talking to you. I had to be in Santa Barbara anyway. It was no trouble."

"Is that it? No trouble?"

"Not really. I know I scared you with that note. Sometimes even FBI agent's have feelings. Besides, I'll tell you something."

"What's that?

"I've been with the Bureau for 27 years now."

"You don't look that old." Actually, he did. But it couldn't hurt to flatter the FBI.

"I turned 51 last month." He had that far off look in his eyes again. I nodded to keep him going.

"It gets ugly sometimes. This business. Not as much as you'd think, but sometimes. It wears on you after a while."

Could FBI agents have feelings? Nah.

"You know," he mused, "I wonder sometimes what it would have been like if I'd gone into practice instead of going to the FBI." I remembered he was a lawyer too. I only thought of him as an FBI agent.

"You wouldn't have liked it," I said. My own experience made me pretty confident I was right.

"I'm not so sure about that. Here's the thing. I look at that pretty little town you're in. That little house you use as an office."

"So?"

"I envy you."

Chapter 49

We had settled back into our house and things had returned pretty much to normal. In the last few weeks, Gino Bartoletti's indictment and incarceration had made all the major television networks and newspapers. Not one of them had called to interview me. Darn. The Federal government had taken over control of the United Union Pension Fund.

It was good to be back at home and into our routine again. Breakfast at the Lilly Pad. A quiet stroll up to the office at about ten. No gray Mercedes. The only fireplugs were the ones Bruno had christened. He gives a new meaning to the term "peon".

Fee income was down, but psychic income was way up. And I took great pleasure at being the envy of the FBI. Even if I knew better.

Karen looked relaxed. The worry lines had retreated from her lovely eyes. So did Bruno, but then, Bruno always looks relaxed. Except when he's asleep, when he looks oblivious.

I'd made it into the office and was sitting at my desk looking out over the harbor with my binoculars. The balmy weather had brought out new objects of note. Red nosed twins. Plump and round. I assure you, I had no personal interest. Purely an art study. The topless girl was just a passing fanny. But I still hadn't figured out who owned that boat.

The phone rang. I put my binoculars down on the windowsill and swung around in my seat.

"James Harris."

"Mr. Harris?" Why do people always do that? I'd just said I was James Harris. Are they trying to confuse me?

"Here."

"This is Seymour Laskin. I'm the president of the Land Trust for the Central Coast. Do you know who we are?" His voice was thin and reedy. I was getting an uncomfortable image of Clarence Jenkins in my head. I shook it off.

"Don't you buy property and hold land for public use?" I said. See I read the papers. I also had made a $3 donation to them once and I received regular mailings every few days.

"Right."

"How can I help you?"

"We'd like to retain you to handle a transaction for us."

"Fantastic." I smelled money. I waggled my eyebrows. I do a great Groucho imitation. "How did I come to your attention?" I tapped at an imaginary cigar.

"We're well aware of the good work you've done in the Franklin Farms matter."

I sat forward and smiled into my empty office. If anyone had been there, they would have been knocked out. It was a very good smile.

"Great," I said. I was doing well by doing good. What could be better? "Can you tell me what land you're seeking to acquire. I assume it's a piece of land."

"Oh, it's actually Franklin Farms itself."

It suddenly occurred to me I had let our filing slide on Save Our Coast now that we were in the clear. I had a sinking feeling.

"Mr. Laskin, you obviously know I'm representing clients in seeking to overturn the entitlements to the Franklin Farms development. I may have a conflict." Although I prayed to God I didn't.

He chuckled. "Oh, I don't think you'll have a conflict. We're buying the land at a very good price from the United

Union Pension Fund. Something of a distress sale I think. You see, the property can't be developed."

That was good news. "Why?"

"It seems the property is one of the best archeological dig sites ever discovered on Chumash culture. It will take years to explore and archive. Maybe decades."

I'm all for the Indians. Did I mention I had lost money at their casino? I was feeling a deeper fondness for them by the moment.

"Really?" I said. I sounded the soul of innocence. I wonder who could have put the archeologists on to Franklin Farms. Hmm. I'd have to check with Clyde.

"Oh, yes. Upon the completion of the purchase we intend to renounce any development rights. We're going to put in trails and a park. We're even considering a dog park. We think this will be very good for the community."

"As do I," I said in my most lawyer-like voice. "I'm very interested. Would you like some information about my fees?"

The line went quiet.

"Mr. Laskin?"

"I'm here," he said. He hesitated. "Mr. Harris, we were hoping . . ." He paused.

"Yes," I said.

"Considering the good work you've done for the community with respect to Franklin Farms already . . ." He paused again.

"Yes," I said more anxiously.

"Well, we assumed . . ., Rather we hoped . . ."

"Yes." This time I knew what was coming.

"That you might do this on a pro bono basis."

"Oy". That's a Jewish term. It's "yo" backwards.

Chapter 50

Our Assemblyperson spoke.

"We are gathered here today . . ." And so on and so forth.

Our Congressperson spoke. "And I wish that every day ..."

And our State Senator spoke. "We need others to heed ..."

And our Mayor spoke. "We cannot thank enough . . ."

I thought his speech was the best. He hit it right on the button. "Enough". The ceremony had already been going on for more than 45 minutes although it seemed like forever.

It was hot in mid-July, even with an on-shore breeze. The sun was bright in the clear air. I felt my shirt sticking to my back. I shifted in my seat a little to try to let my shirt dry.

The ranch house at Franklin Farms looked rather woebegone. Empty houses have a sad aura with their blank eyes. We were sitting in white plastic folding chairs by the pool where Janet Mason had died. A podium had been set up at one end. The local television station was covering the ceremony.

Finally Seymour Laskin, of the Land Trust, stood as the mayor introduced him. He was a large man, over 6' tall, maybe 6'2", with a halo of white hair around his bald head.

He stepped to the podium and adjusted the mike. He tapped it twice. It squawked in protest. He leaned in to get closer.

"Good afternoon." His thin and reedy voice carried through the mike. Not at all the voice of so large a man. "Thank you, Mayor Porter. We of the Land Trust are very pleased to have been able to acquire this wonderful property and preserve it forever as a piece of our heritage which we will be able to pass on to our children and our children's children. We could not have done it without the efforts of Congressperson Roberta Grace . . ." he nodded to the Congressperson, "Assemblyman Morton Pels, State Senator John Perry and Mayor Sidney Porter." More nods. I was concerned he was going to hurt himself. Then he paused. There was a polite round of applause.

"Nor could we have done it without the generosity of so many of you in the community." Another smattering of applause. "Among those who have contributed so much, I would like to especially thank James Emerson Harris." He paused. No applause. Hey, come on.

"Mr. Harris not only led the fight to challenge the entitlements for the Franklin Farms development. . ." The mayor didn't even have the decency to blush at the way he'd pushed the entitlements through, but then, he's a politician. "But he also assisted us, on a pro bono basis, in obtaining this property for the Land Trust and so, for you and your community."

Karen, who was sitting beside me, squeezed my hand and looked proud. It almost made it worth all the free work. She looked beautiful in a green, bare shouldered sundress that set off her eyes. Have I mentioned her green eyes? Bruno sat in her lap, taking in the new vista.

"Mr. Harris, would you step forward and escort the guest of honor to the podium." I did as I was told. I'm good at that.

"I would like to now officially name this portion of this beautiful property," a three or four acre parcel that had been marked off with red ribbons, "in honor of our recipient today," a dramatic pause. This guy really had it down with dramatic pauses. "The Bruno Harris Dog Park." Thunderous applause.

Bruno looked pleased. He wagged his tail. Then he lifted his leg and peed on the side of the podium. More thunderous applause. I couldn't wait to see the evening news.

I guess it was being back up at Franklin Farms. Particularly seeing the swimming pool. Karen and I hadn't talked a lot about the whole mess. It was sort of by mutual agreement. But after the ceremony, we had gone to Mario's for dinner. It was around six and it was still light outside. But Mario's was cool and dark. It was empty. We were early.

Maria made an exception and allowed Bruno to sit under the table. I mean, given the honor that had been bestowed on him that afternoon, it was understandable. Yes, he wanted a chair, but Maria drew the line there.

Bruno seemed happy nonetheless. Maria had given him a bowl of water and a plate of meatballs. I ordered two Hakke Becks, poured his water out and poured him a beer. Not a beer, of course. A non-alcoholic beer. We think he's too young to drink. He seemed happy anyway, lapping at the Hakke Beck. He's got his tongue work down pat.

Karen seemed relaxed. Mellow. In the dimness, her green dress had taken on a different hue. She sipped at her Zager Reserve Chardonnay.

I was the one who brought up the murders. Well, we only knew about one for sure, but from what Agent Leary said, I was pretty certain Guy Mason's death wasn't an accident. I'll bet his brakes failed. Not the best dinner conversation. But it had to surface, get acknowledged, so we could move on.

"It was kind of creepy being back up at the house," I said. "Have you thought about Janet Mason?"

Karen took a sip of wine and nodded. But her eyes didn't leave my face.

"What do you think it was all about?" As I've said, Karen's the deep one. "I don't mean how she manipulated everyone. I mean about suing for divorce."

"Jimmy, Janet had it all figured out. You just don't see it, do you?" She said it in a low voice so that I had to lean forward to hear her. She put her glass back on the table and moved her index finger absently around the rim.

Okay, I'm stupid. But I'm a man. That must be some excuse. "I don't get it."

Maria bustled over with two plates of pasta. She set them in front of us with a flourish. "Mangia," she said. Then she stood still. Karen and I looked up at her expectantly. "I see you on the 5 o'clock news, Jimmy. You look good. Mario and me, we want to give you this dinner on us."

I smiled up at Maria. Karen handled the "thank yous". She does that well. She's gracious. I tend to be a smart ass. I'll bet you didn't know that. I keep it well hidden.

"Why do you think Janet turned down a $2 million settlement?" Karen asked, as Maria walked away to greet two more early guests.

"I told you. I don't know. Maybe she knew about the insurance?" I dug into my pasta.

"Maybe she did. But the insurance was worthless," Karen said. She was using the Socratic method. You learn from answering questions. At least some people do. Karen should have been an attorney. But then, if she was one, I might be out of business.

"Unless Guy Mason was dead," I said. I said it around a mouthful of food. I'm a growing boy.

"Which he became." Karen picked up her glass of wine in both hands and looked at me over the rim. Her look was intense. It's amazing to me how she can ignore food. "What

301

would have happened if Guy Mason had been killed and she was his wife?"

"I guess if there had been any suspicious circumstances, she would be the prime suspect. Being the wife." The police always suspect the wife. I knew that from watching television. "Particularly if there were no other assets in the estate."

"But if she were suing him for divorce?"

"Why don't you eat your pasta before it gets cold," I said. It was a diversion. I needed time to think.

Karen took a small forkful and chewed daintily. She kept looking at me. "So?"

"She'd be in the clear," I said. "And she wouldn't want to settle before Guy Mason's death because she needed to be his wife to be the beneficiary of his estate." The penny dropped. What a neat alibi. Me. "We really got taken, didn't we?" I can use the Socratic method too. Usually, when you do that you're supposed to know the answer. So this was the exception.

Karen may have noticed that I said "we" got taken. I just wanted her to feel included. Karen raised her eyebrow at me. Something else she does well. It must be the practice she gets.

I lifted another forkful of pasta to my mouth and dripped sauce onto my shirt. "Damn." I dipped the tip of my napkin into my water glass and rubbed ineffectively at the spot. This wasn't the first time this had happened. Karen doesn't even comment anymore. At least not verbally. Her eyebrows do the talking. Women seem to be able to do that. Then she started to respond to my question.

Bruno, at that point, gave out a loud belch. His sense of timing is impeccable.

We looked at each other and started to laugh. "Maybe not," Karen said. She lifted up the edge of the red checked tablecloth and looked at Bruno. I thought there was love in her eyes.

"Do you feel differently?" she asked him. Bruno didn't respond. He only looked at her and wagged his tail. I personally think he didn't have an opinion. He just wanted attention. He still hadn't gotten his fill of adulation. Didn't he know he was only entitled to 15 minutes? Maybe I should teach him to tell time.

Karen dropped the tablecloth back into place and looked up. "Feel better?"

I was looking at Karen. I didn't really, but at least it all fell into place. Not where I wanted. But into place. And, of course, I was the schmuck with a pen.

Only Janet Mason had gotten it wrong. I shuddered at what would have happened to us if the scheme had gone down like Janet had figured. I didn't think they'd have wanted any witnesses. That wasn't a good thought. Maybe now I didn't feel so bad about Janet.

I looked across at Karen. She had the wineglass to her lips. She had eaten a thimbleful of pasta. The candlelight flickered off of the golden wine. I don't ever remember her being more beautiful. I was feeling drunk on sobriety.

"Will you marry me?" I said. It was impulsive. Even impetuous. But it was out there. Maybe I'd had too much Hakke Beck.

She put down her wineglass and gave me a serious look. I sensed I needed to do something. This was different. There was a chance here. I seized it.

"If you'll marry me, Bruno can be my best man." There. I took my best shot. Bruno poked his nose out at the sound of his name.

"You feel that close to Bruno?" Karen said. I reached over and picked up her hand from the table. I turned it palm up and kissed it lightly. I whispered, "Yes, I do."

Her face was radiant. I could see the love in her eyes.

She said, "Well, in that case, I guess Bruno and I won't be able to run away together. So, why not?"

That caught me up short. "You? Bruno? What?" You talk about mixed emotions. Mixed emotions are when your mother-in-law drives your new Porsche off a cliff.

She smiled mischievously.

"Is that a 'yes'," I said. "You'll marry me?"

She gave me a nod that was as big as all the world for such a very small gesture.

She said, "I will."

"Karen . . .," I started. She held up her hand to stop me. She executed a dramatic pause worthy of Seymour Laskin.

"Of course, I'll want a pre-nuptial agreement," she said.
She was kidding. Right?

The End

ABOUT THE AUTHOR

David L. Gersh, the celebrated author (he celebrates quite often) is a recovering corporate lawyer whose long and checkered career started with his first deal, when he was sent to the great metropolis of New York for two days at the behest of his boss, Mickey Rudin. It was to participate on behalf of Frank Sinatra in the sale of a bedraggled Hollywood movie studio to a small funeral home company (now known as Time-Warner). He returned two and a half months later, sidetracking a promising future as an impoverished poet.

He attended Harvard Law School quite by accident. He is now a retired partner of one of the great international law firms, Paul Hastings, which he still loves dearly, from afar.

He lives in Santa Barbara, California.